Also by Penny Joelson:

I Have No Secrets

Nominated for the CILIP Carnegie
Children's Book Award 2018
Winner of the Worcestershire Teen Book Award
Winner of the Leeds Book Award

GIRL IN THE WINDOW

PENNY JOELSON

First published in Great Britain in 2018 by Electric Monkey,
an imprint of Egmont UK Limited
The Yellow Building, 1 Nicholas Road, London W11 4AN

Text copyright © 2018 Penny Joelson

ISBN 978 1 4052 8616 9

The moral rights of the author have been asserted

67156/001

www.egmont.co.uk

A CIP catalogue record for this title is available from the British Library

Typeset by Avon DataSet Ltd, Bidford on Avon, Warwickshire
Printed and bound in Great Britain by the CPI Group

For Cherry

'There's no one coming to look for me because no one even knows I've gone missing.'
Unrest (2017)

No one sees me. I am a ghost. I am invisible. Life for me stopped still, one day — when I was not expecting it. Out there, I know that life goes on, that time moves forward, but it does so without me. I know I shouldn't but I want to look once more — to take a peek out through the window at a world that is not mine. Do I dare?

1

It's dark when I see her. I'm closing my curtains, ready for bed — and there's a woman hurrying along our street towards the bus stop. There's something intense about the way she's moving. She darts like a bird. It's as if she's rushing to catch a bus — but there's no bus there and no one waiting. The street is quiet. I'm not sure why I keep watching but I do. She's skinny — with long, dark hair, maybe in her late teens, early twenties. She's barely more than a silhouette in the darkness, but as she passes the street light, it casts her elongated shadow across the road. The glow highlights the long, thin cardigan she's wearing. She pulls it tight around her, head bent against the chill November wind, but she goes past the bus stop without slowing down.

I see her glance round briefly as two cars pass. Now a silver car's coming. It swerves and stops alongside her. Her head turns sharply. At the same moment, a man jumps out from the passenger side. He grabs the

woman by the arm. She pulls away. They're struggling
— at least, that's what it looks like. Within seconds,
he's opened the back door of the car and she's in. He
bangs the door shut and jumps back in the front. The
car drives off, disappearing around the corner.

It happened so fast — but I'm certain she didn't
want to get into that car. The man was dragging her —
forcing her in. I think he even had his hand over her
mouth. I can barely believe it. I keep replaying it in my
mind. My heart is thudding like a bass drum.

I'm staring out at the now empty street, still in
shock, when a movement catches my eye. I look up at
the house across the road, the window opposite mine.
The curtain moved, I'm sure it did. Someone was
looking out. Did they see what I just saw?

Should I call the police? There's a couple in that
house across the road — if one of them saw, maybe
they've gone to call the police right now. But even
so . . .

'Mum!' I yell, grabbing my phone. 'Mum!'

She's watching TV downstairs and I don't think
she heard me. Anyway, I don't need her to tell me
what to do, and I shouldn't wait. I shouldn't let them
get too far away.

I sit on my bed and call 999. My hand is shaking. I've never done this before – never dealt with a real emergency. I ask for police.

There's a calm voice at the end of the phone – a man's voice. He listens and then starts asking me questions.

I give my name, Kasia Novak, and address, 47 New Weald Lane.

'Did you get the car registration number?' he asks.

I feel instantly devastated. Why didn't I? 'I'm sorry. No. It was all so fast,' I tell him.

'Don't worry – you did the right thing to call. Any information you can give us will help. Can you describe the car?'

'It was silver – a hatchback . . . I'm not sure what kind.'

I can describe the woman but I didn't see the driver and only have a vague impression of the man who jumped out. I'm a useless witness.

'Silver hatchback,' he repeats, as if he's writing it down. 'We'll get someone on to it straight away.'

'Oh, and I think someone else might have seen it – across the road,' I tell him. 'I think there was someone at the window upstairs. They might even have called you too. It was number forty-eight.'

'We'll speak to them. Thank you for reporting the incident. Please call us if you remember any other details.' He gives me another phone number and a case number, which I write on a scrap of paper.

I have a sinking feeling as I put the phone down. I wish I'd got the car reg. Maybe whoever was watching across the road did. I hope so.

'Mum! Mum!' I call again. She still doesn't hear. I want to tell her. I need to tell her. I stand up, holding on to the window ledge for support, and then walk slowly out into the hallway, one hand pressed against the wall. My glands are throbbing in my neck and my legs are throbbing too – a constant dull, familiar ache.

'Mum!' No reply. I clutch the banister and put one foot gingerly on the top step. I've been thinking about trying to go downstairs for a few days, but I know now isn't really the right moment. I'm too shaken up – on top of everything else.

'Kasia! What are you doing?' Mum appears at the bottom of the stairs, looking up at me with concern.

My legs give way and I sit down on the top step. 'I was calling you. You didn't hear. I thought I'd come down . . .'

Mum's up beside me now, tutting and holding out her arm. 'You look very pale, *mój aniele*. Come on, time for bed. How many times do I have to tell you to take it slowly, not do too much too quickly? Just getting out of bed is a big achievement. You're clearly not up to trying the stairs. You should text me if I don't hear you.'

I'm too tired to argue, but I want to prove her wrong. I'm so fed up with being in my bedroom all the time. Tomorrow, I think to myself. Maybe I'll try tomorrow. But I still want to tell her what just happened.

Mum helps me into bed and sits on the edge as I tell her all about what I saw. She's really shocked.

'Kasia, how awful! Are you sure?'

'I think so . . .'

Mum touches my hand gently. 'You did the right thing to phone the police. Now settle down and get some sleep. You look exhausted.'

She goes back down and I lie in my bed, staring at the same four walls. It's ten weeks since I've been downstairs.

2

I'm sitting by my bedroom window, waiting for Ellie to come round after school like she promised. She's the only one of my friends that still does. The street is busy with cars on the school run and kids walking home. It looks so normal, it's hard to believe what I saw last night actually happened. I've been playing it over in my mind all day. It feels like a bad dream, not something real. Where is that woman now – what happened to her? I wonder if someone has reported her missing.

I glance at the house across the road. Have the police spoken to them yet? Was someone looking out last night, or did I just imagine I saw the curtain move?

At the bus stop, groups in school uniform stand chatting. A toddler in a buggy has pulled off one shoe and is chewing it. I watch as she takes the shoe out of her mouth and flings it under the bench. Her mother is sitting staring at her phone and hasn't noticed.

The bus comes, blocking my view, and when it pulls out the people, including the woman and the buggy have gone, but I can still see the purple shoe sticking out sadly from under the bench.

A man in his twenties with dark hair and glasses arrives at the bus stop and kicks at the shoe curiously. I start making up a kind of Cinderella story, where the man takes the shoe and puts a photo of it on a Facebook group, and the woman comes forward gratefully to claim it. Turns out they're both single and when they meet to hand over the shoe, it's love at first sight.

I see a police car coming along the road and it pulls into a parking bay further down the road. Is this to do with last night? At first I think they want to ask me more questions but the police officer walks quickly up to the door of number forty-eight. I watch eagerly and see the front door open. The policeman talks to the woman and I can see her shaking her head.

Once the door closes, the policeman knocks on the doors of the houses on either side, but no one is home. Then he crosses the road. He's coming here! The doorbell rings. I wish I could run down and answer it but I have to wait for Mum to do it. I hear her talking to the policeman and I wonder if she'll bring him upstairs, but she says goodbye after only a minute and then comes up.

'What did he say?' I ask eagerly.

'They haven't found out anything about an abduction, Kasia,' Mum tells me. 'No one has been reported missing and no one else contacted them about it. He said the people at forty-eight saw nothing. They were both downstairs watching television.'

'I thought someone was there, watching,' I say, 'upstairs – in the room opposite mine. I saw the curtain move, like someone was peeping out.'

Mum shrugs. 'The police are looking into it. If there's anything to discover, I'm sure they'll find it.'

Mum goes back down and I'm still waiting for Ellie. Where is she? I'm suddenly worried she won't turn up. I'm dying to tell her what I saw. Maybe I should have texted her, so she'd know I had something to talk about for once.

Just when I think she's really not coming, I finally spot her, hurrying along the pavement, her ponytail bobbing up and down. I can see she's trying to be quick but it feels like a hundred years before she turns into our gate and rings the doorbell. I hear Mum's footsteps on the hall floor as she goes to let Ellie in, and then more, lighter steps as Ellie pads up the stairs.

She comes into my bedroom with a beaming smile and two plates of Mum's apple cake. I take a deep sniff of the lovely cinnamon smell that has been drifting through the house, making my mouth water.

'Sorry I'm a bit late – it's all been happening today!' she says, plonking herself on the edge of my bed and handing me a plate.

'Tell me!' I say. I like hearing what's going on at school. It makes me feel more part of it, although it also sometimes makes me sad.

'At lunchtime Serene got into a fight with Bethany,' Ellie tells me. 'A proper punch-up – Bethany pulled Serene's hair and a whole clump came out! I saw it in her hand! It was over some boy. I don't even know who.'

I feel a pang. I hope it wasn't Josh. He's a boy I like in the year above – a boy with ocean-blue eyes and a husky voice. I can't imagine him with Bethany or Serene, though.

'Then,' Ellie continues, 'Dimitri and Rafi were messing about in maths and Mr Treaker completely lost it and slammed a ruler on the desk so hard it flipped in the air and hit Serene in the face! She had to go to the medical room and now she's got a massive black eye, too!'

'Ohhh, poor Serene!' I exclaim, though I can't help laughing.

'We shouldn't laugh,' says Ellie, giggling too, 'but she's always so obsessed with how she looks – and I'm sure she started that fight!'

'Anyway, listen,' she says, when we've both finally stopped laughing. 'I have news you're going to want to hear!'

I want to say, 'So do I!' but she's made me curious. Her eyes are shining, her smile even broader. It must be something good, really good.

'What?' I ask. I take a bite of cake and lean forwards. 'What is it?'

'Guess,' she says. 'It's about you . . .'

I hesitate. For one crazy moment I wonder if it's something to do with Josh. Maybe he asked after me . . .

'I can see your dreamy eyes!' she teases. 'No, it isn't about *Josh*, Kasia!'

'OK.' I feel myself blushing. Ellie knows me too well. 'I can't guess – you'll have to tell me.'

'You're going to love this!' she insists, stuffing

rather too much cake into her mouth. 'Ooh, your mum makes the best cake!'

'Tell,' I demand, rolling my eyes because now she can't speak. She swallows and grins at me.

'Remember that story you wrote – that one that was like a mash-up of *Hunger Games* and *Titanic*?'

'Sort of. That was ages ago – before I was ill. What about it?'

'It was sooooo good – Miss Giles said she might enter it for a competition. Do you remember?'

It's weird thinking back. I was first ill in June so it must have been May when I wrote that story. I remember the bustle of our English class and the way the room went silent as I started to read my story aloud. I remember even Rafi and Dimitri had their eyes fixed on me as I read. They clapped too at the end, along with everyone else. Miss Giles was full of praise, saying I could be an author one day.

But that was six months ago, when we were all in Year 9. Now the class have moved up – they are Year 10s, with a different English teacher, working for their GCSEs. I don't even know which classroom they are in or what time the lesson is.

'Kasia?'

I realise I haven't answered her. 'Yes,' I tell Ellie. 'I remember.'

Well, listen to this . . . she *did* enter it – and you won! First prize!'

'*What?* You're joking!'

'Look – here's the proof.'

Ellie scrabbles in her rucksack and pulls out an envelope that has already been opened. It's addressed to Miss Giles at school. She slips the letter out, unfolds it and hands it to me, pointing.

'See – First Prize awarded to Kasia Novak.'

'Wow!' I say. I've never won anything before in my life – except a tiny rubber duck at a tombola when I was five. It used to glow in the dark.

'Miss Giles is well chuffed,' says Ellie. 'She came running up to me in the corridor.'

'What did I win?' I ask, scanning the text. I'm hoping it's money, though I know it's unlikely to be much. With Mum not working, every little helps.

'You get to go to an award ceremony in a theatre,' she tells me. 'Oh . . .'

Her voice falters and she looks at me, her hand covering her mouth.

'When and where?' I demand.

'It's not until February – and it's in central London somewhere. Maybe by then . . .'

I'm conscious of my throbbing glands and my heart's pulsing too. I feel weak but I also feel a surge of determination. I look Ellie in the eye and tell her, 'I *will* be better. I can't miss something like that! And I'm going to get back to school, Els.'

'Have you been downstairs yet?' Ellie asks.

'No, but I'm going down for dinner today. Don't tell Mum – she doesn't know! I want to surprise her.'

'Really? That's great!'

Ellie's being a supportive best friend but I can see she still looks doubtful. She knows how long it is since I've been downstairs.

We read the letter again, together. I still can't take it all in. 'Oh, look, you get fifty pounds worth of book tokens too, and a hundred pounds' worth of books for the school,' Ellie tells me.

'Miss Giles will be pleased about that!' I smile.

'Look, I've got to go,' says Ellie. 'Tons of homework. I'll try and come again on Thursday.'

It's only after she's gone that I realise I forgot to tell her about last night.

3

My words to Ellie may have sounded brave and determined but I know it's not going to be that easy. I am not in Year 10 with all my friends but, back in September, I did try to be. Nobody knew I was going to be so ill for so long.

I remember Ellie waiting for me at the school gate, a beaming smile spreading across her face when she spotted me.

'I'm so glad you made it!' she told me. 'I didn't want to start the new school year without you!'

'Same here,' I said, waving Mum off in the car. I meant it too. I'd always been determined to be well by the end of the summer holidays. I knew that I wasn't OK, though. I was achy, weak and in pain. I'm sure Mum knew it too but we both wanted to believe that once I got to school I'd feel better and everything would somehow, magically, go back to normal.

'Come on, let's get in,' said Ellie. 'Don't want to

be late on the first day!'

We walked to the main entrance. I felt so weird and wobbly, as if the ground underneath me was moving. I tried to ignore the dull ache in my legs and the swollen glands making my neck stiff and uncomfortable.

Inside, everything seemed different. The corridor looked so much longer. Erin and Tilly rushed up to say hi, and Tilly tried to hug me. It hurt, but I didn't like to say so. They were clearly pleased to see me back, chattering and asking me questions.

'I thought it was just tonsillitis,' said Erin. 'How come it took you so long to get better?'

'The doctor said I had post-viral fatigue,' I explained. 'I still felt ill even though the infection had gone. No idea why. It just happens sometimes. Did you have a good summer?'

'We went camping in France,' she told me. 'The first week was amazing but then it rained the rest of the time! I never want to go camping again.'

She kept talking, telling me about all the other things she'd been doing. I zoned out. People were talking all around me too. I couldn't take the noise. Surely school never used to be this loud? As we reached the stairs to our form room I looked up and was overcome by panic. It was a flight of stairs – a flight I'd climbed every day for years but now it looked like a mountain. How would I ever get up there? And the crowds – I couldn't bear all the people swarming around me. I suddenly felt so fragile, as if I was a delicate flower about to be trodden into the ground.

'You are OK, aren't you?' Ellie asked.

'Not really,' I told her.

'You can use the lift if you need to.'

I did, but I felt weird, embarrassed, standing waiting for it. The lift is for disabled students. I'm not disabled. When I got out on the first floor, I was sure everyone was staring at me.

I sat down with relief in my form room, listening to more holiday stories, with people coming up to say they were so happy I was better and how I looked fine. I didn't feel fine, even sitting down. When I looked at my Year 10 timetable, I had a sinking feeling. I even asked Ellie, 'Have they put more lessons in this year?' and she looked at me like I was mad.

'French first!' she said cheerfully. 'Look, we've got Madame Dupont! She's the best.'

I like Madame Dupont and I like French, but I didn't smile back because the room was on the other side of the school. The thought of having to stand up and walk down more corridors, packed with students, already felt too much.

I made it to French but within minutes I felt so ill I couldn't sit any more – I had to lie down. Ellie took me to the medical room. The nurse called my Mum straight away.

I'd lasted thirty-seven minutes in Year 10.

Now, I stand at the top of the stairs, looking down. I imagine I'm an Olympic skier at the peak of a challenging slope. The previous contender has been taken off in an ambulance. I don't know the extent of her injuries but, after checks, the organisers have declared the course safe. I am not so sure.

I cling to the banister, aware that I am holding my breath as I put one foot tentatively forward. Then the other. I'm getting into a rhythm, but halfway down I feel light-headed and my legs feel like they're going to give way. I haven't been downstairs since that day – the first day of term, 2 September, when I tried to go back to school. But I am starting to improve.

When I didn't get better after tonsillitis, Mum and Dad were constantly trying to get me to do more and

I had to make them understand that I couldn't. Dad actually thought I'd got lazy from being ill in bed. Mum thought it must be depression or anxiety, especially when she took me to the doctor who did blood tests that all came back clear. The doctor said it was possible I had post-viral fatigue, and mentioned chronic fatigue syndrome or CFS, though it's more often known as ME. It stands for Myalgic Encephalomyelitis. That was probably the reason I was taking so long to recover. But I don't think Mum and Dad realised exactly what that meant, or how long it might take. I didn't either. I know now, though.

I. Know. Now.

People can be ill for years with this. Some people never get better. I'm not going to be one of them. I can't.

I've been thinking about trying to come downstairs for a couple of weeks — but I've been so scared of getting stuck halfway, or not feeling well enough to go back up again, that I've been too frightened to even try. I know I have to get over this fear, but it's based on real experience. I only have to do the smallest thing and it wipes me out completely. Already I need to sit down, but that's OK. Now it is as far to go back up as it is to keep going, and down is definitely easier.

I start going again, before I panic. And then I've made it! I'm down! I'm a little giddy, but I'm here.

I wait for a few moments to get steady, then I take a deep breath and stroll casually into the kitchen. I'm almost surprised that it looks exactly the same. I feel like so much time has passed that Mum might have a new tablecloth or kettle or something. She's busy at the stove, stirring something in a saucepan. The smell is like a life force to me. I feel stronger just being close to it.

'Hi, Mum! That stew smells delish.'

She nearly drops the spoon in the pan.

'Kasia!' She rests the spoon on a plate and flings her arms around me. She knows to be gentle. She lets go of me and rubs her eyes.

'Don't cry, Mum!' I tease.

'It's onions, just the onions,' she says with a smile. 'You should have told me you wanted to try coming down. I would have helped you, *mój aniele!* Do you feel OK? Are you sure it wasn't too much? Come – sit. After all those stairs you must sit. Let me get you a drink.'

She brings me a cushion for the hard, plastic chair.

My whole body is so sensitive these days. I'm already starting to feel weak, but I don't say anything about it. I hope Dad gets home soon. I'm not sure how long I'm going to last.

I glance at the photos on the fridge. Me and Dad making silly faces, Mum posing on a bridge, a picture of my aunt and uncle in Poland. There's one missing — the one of me and my brother Marek. I'm sad, but not surprised. Dad and Marek haven't spoken since he dropped out of uni and went off around Europe.

Dad is home early to my relief — and the expression of delight on his face as his large frame and bald head fill the kitchen doorway makes it all worthwhile.

He's still in his work clothes, dirty from his day at the building site, but he does his funny version of a traditional Polish celebration dance round the small kitchen. Mum hastily moves crockery and pans out of the way so nothing goes flying and I am laughing so much it actually hurts.

'*Moje kochanie,*' he says, gently stroking my hair. 'It's so lovely to have you down here and not exiled upstairs. I hope this is a sign of good things to come.'

'I only wish Marek was here to see you too,' Mum says, sighing.

'So do I,' I tell her, getting a pang as I imagine my brother here too, grinning and high-fiving me.

Dad tuts scornfully.

'Dad!' I protest.

'Let's not spoil the evening talking about *him*,' Dad says firmly. 'Give me two ticks to get changed and when I come down, we'll talk about something else, something happier.'

Mum winks at me when he's gone and picks up her phone from the worktop. 'I'll take a photo of you at the table and we'll WhatsApp it to him,' she says quietly. 'Marek will be so pleased.'

Dad comes back down and Mum serves up.

'Well, what's new?' Dad asks.

'We had a visit from a policeman,' Mum says. 'Very handsome he was!'

'I hope he didn't stay long then,' Dad teases. 'This about what you saw the night before, Kasia?'

I nod and Mum tells Dad what he said.

'I hope they find the woman,' I say. 'I just want to know she's OK.'

'Well, you did the right thing reporting it,' Dad says to me. 'The rest is up to them.'

I know Dad's right. There's nothing else I can do.

'I thought we were going to talk about happy things,' says Mum.

'Hey, yes! How about this for a happy thing?' I say, smiling.

I tell them about winning the writing competition and they are both thrilled. Dad gets up to do another celebration dance but Mum tells him to stop or he'll get indigestion.

'I want to get well enough to go the award ceremony,' I tell them. 'And I want you both to come with me.'

'I'll do my best,' says Dad, 'but you know how things are. It isn't always easy for me to get time off. It's a big project, this sheltered housing, and we're a month behind already. Hopefully by then we will be back on track.'

Although I want Dad to be there, I'm mainly pleased that he's not even questioning the idea that I'll be able to go myself.

'It's exciting Kasia, but you need to be careful,' says Mum. 'We'll have to see how you are nearer the time.'

Mum may be more realistic, but I prefer Dad's optimism. Although as she speaks I realise that the room is starting to spin. I don't want Mum to be right, but in the end I have to tell her. 'I need to lie down.'

'Let me help you back up to bed,' she says. 'You've done really well, but that's enough for now. I can bring you up dessert if you'd like some.'

As I stand up, panic rises in my chest. 'Mum – I don't think I can do it – I don't think I can get back upstairs. I need to lie down now!'

'Lie on the sofa for a minute,' Dad suggests. 'Here – take my arm.'

He helps me into the front room where I collapse on to the sofa. I still feel like I'm on a boat in a storm and the panic is overtaking me. I want my bed – I want to be in my room.

After twenty minutes, I don't feel any better. Dad sits down beside me.

'I want to go to bed,' I tell him.

'I'll help you, *kotku*.' He holds out his arm.

I shake my head. 'I can't stand up, Dad.'

'Lucky you have a strong father then,' he says. He's standing now, smiling and holding out both arms.

'Dad!' I exclaim. He hasn't carried me anywhere since I was about five years old.

'I've carried heavier weights around the site today,'

he assures me. 'Look at these muscles.'

Before I can protest he has me in his arms and is lifting me. Much as I hate being treated like a child, I enjoy feeling safe and warm and held and I am more grateful than anything when he lowers me gently on to my bed.

4

I can't get up the next day or the next and, apart from crawling to the bathroom next door, I don't try to do much else. The only other thing I stand to do is draw the curtains – open in the morning and closed at night. I know Mum would do it, but I want to look out – remind myself that there is a world out there.

This evening I look across the road and I can see a light on upstairs in the room opposite mine at number forty-eight. Someone is drawing the curtains there too. I briefly catch a glimpse of the figure but it doesn't look like the man or woman who live there. It's someone skinnier – a girl, I think. Was it her I saw in the window the other night, when the woman was abducted?

Now that I've been downstairs, my small bedroom is feeling even smaller than it did before. Lying in my bed, all I can see is the pale pink walls, painted when I was six, matching pale pink curtains, my wicker chair by the window, and a white desk and white wardrobe against the wall. On the wall is a small picture — a Polish village scene with a girl outside a church — that once belonged to my grandmother. And I have a tiny bedside shelf for my glass of water, phone and clock.

My duvet cover makes my room look more grown up — it's silky pink with splashes of purple on it. There's no room for my cello in here and maybe that's for the best. It's downstairs in the corner of the lounge and I am glad not to have to look at it and be constantly reminded that I can't even pick it up, let alone play it.

Marek's room is a little bigger than mine and Dad asked if I wanted to swap when Marek went to uni. But I didn't — his room is painted black and orange, which would have taken many coats of paint to cover. And anyway, I didn't want to think of Marek as having left home. I thought he'd be back in the long holidays, and even when he'd finished uni. I'm still glad his room is as he left it, waiting for him to come back.

I lie in bed, sleeping, listening to podcasts and audiobooks on my phone, meditating and thinking of ideas for stories. Then my mind turns to Josh. I like him so much. Only Ellie knows how I feel. I wish I'd had the courage to say something to him while I was well. I kept hoping he'd speak to me, but maybe he's shy. He's in the year above me but we were both in the orchestra – I could have said something then, but I didn't. He's probably going out with someone else by now and I wouldn't blame him. He has no idea how I feel about him, so it's not as if he'd be waiting for me to get better.

I get a message from Marek. He's seen Mum's photo of me sitting downstairs, and his message is full of excited smiley emojis, along with a photo of a frozen pizza, with the caption 'My job is cheese sprinkling!'

Dad had better not see that!

I reply, telling him about the writing competition, and get more excited smiley emojis back. I think about telling him about the abduction, but I'm too tired to text that much.

I lie back and think about the award ceremony again. I just have to get well enough to go. I *must*.

A few days later, I'm feeling a bit better. I don't feel like attempting the stairs again but I'm mostly OK being out of bed. I sit on the floor and open my chest of drawers, just for something to do. There I find the

Get Well card with the cheerful yellow sunflowers on it. I open it and run my finger over Josh's signature. I wonder if he ever thinks about me now. The card is also signed by the other twenty-four members of the orchestra but his is the only name in there that really matters to me. He's an amazing violin player and when we'd finished orchestra practice he used to meet my eyes sometimes and smile. I'm sure something would have happened between us one day.

I put the card back in the drawer. My legs are hurting from sitting on the floor but I don't feel too bad otherwise so I stand stiffly and sit on my wicker chair by the window, looking out. I still feel like I'm on a boat — but it's a gentle rowing boat now. I watch as the woman at number forty-eight comes out, bumping the grey buggy with a rain cover over it, down the steps to the street. She hurries off up the road and I glance up to the window above. There's no one there.

It's raining heavily now — big drops streaking down my window like bars, reminding me of the prison my room has become. It's hard to see through the rain, but I try. There's no one looking out across the road. Cars splash past in the big puddle by the bus stop.

The haziness makes everything seem unreal. It's like the rain is trying to wash away what I saw – washing it all away, wiping the slate clean, a fresh start.

I can't remember it clearly now. Maybe none of it happened at all. But if it *did*, what happened to that woman? I can't help wondering about her.

It's a week later when I pluck up the courage – and have the energy – to go downstairs again. And it's fine! I stay for a whole meal, and also get back upstairs by myself too. I do it again, each day stretching it out a little longer, and I don't have any ill effects.

I feel full of hope – I'm finally getting better – and I want to do more.

Mum comes into the living room, waving a parcel at me. 'I'm just popping next door,' she tells me. 'The delivery man left it here this morning, when he couldn't get an answer.'

'I could take it,' I offer.

Mum looks at me in surprise. 'Are you sure you feel up to it?'

'It's only next door. And it would be good to get outside. Let me, Mum. I'll be fine.'

'OK,' says Mum, but she's looking very doubtful.

'Is it forty-three?' I ask her. 'Won't they be at work?'

'No – forty-seven,' says Mum. 'Mrs Gayatri.'

'How did she manage to miss a parcel?' I comment. 'She never goes out.'

'She does sometimes,' Mum says with a shrug. 'Perhaps she was having a nap or just didn't hear the door.'

'OK. I won't be long,' I tell Mum.

It's weird putting on outdoor shoes when I've worn nothing but slippers for months, and I've rarely been out of bed enough to even need them. My shoes feel hard and uncomfortable in contrast.

'Put your coat on,' Mum fusses. 'And your scarf.'

'It's only next door!' I say, but I do it anyway.

I take the small package and step out of the house – so happy to actually be outside. I wonder what Mrs Gayatri has ordered. It's rectangular but not heavy. We don't see our neighbours very often. There's a young couple on the other side, at number forty-three. We only know their names because they sometimes have parcels delivered while they're at work, and Mum takes them in. I don't remember Mrs G ever having a delivery before, though.

We don't see her much either, though I used to sometimes see her weeding her front path. She's the only person round here who has pots and flowers and bushes out the front. She's not very chatty, but she always has a smile and says hello if we pass her. Of course, since I've been ill I've only seen her from my window, on her rare walks up the road to the shops.

The cool breeze makes my cheeks tingle as I stand on Mrs G's front step and ring her bell. I feel a buzz of excitement and breathe in deeply. It's one step closer to normal life. There's no answer and I wonder if the bell is working. I wait a few moments, try again and then resort to the old-fashioned lion's head knocker. I listen but can hear no sound from inside. The lion's face is snarling at me and I'm about to turn back home because my legs are beginning to throb, which sometimes happens when I'm standing still. Then I hear a small sound – a definite movement from inside.

'Mrs Gayatri?' I call. 'It's me – Kasia from next door. I have a parcel for you.'

The door opens and Mrs Gayatri peers out nervously. She seems more shrunken and wrinkled than I remember, but her eyes are soft and kind.

She smiles. 'Hello, dear. I haven't seen you for

a long time. I wondered if you'd gone away to college.'

'No. I'm fourteen.'

People often think I'm older because I'm tall for my age. I have Dad to thank for that. Mrs G is short – shorter than me.

'I've been ill – I *am* ill. It's ME – Chronic Fatigue Syndrome,' I tell her. 'I get exhausted after I do anything.'

'How awful for you,' she says.

'This is the first time I've been outside for months,' I tell her.

'Goodness, is it really? You poor girl! So, what can I do for you?'

'I've just come to bring you this.' I hold out the parcel. 'The postman left it with us. I'm sorry, I can't stand for very long and I'll have to get back now.'

'Thank you, dear,' she says. 'It's nice to see you. And if you ever fancy a change of scene – or company – you are welcome to pop in. And I mean that.'

I nod and smile. I always thought she liked keeping herself to herself. She doesn't seem to have many visitors. But there's a look of longing in her eyes as she says, 'I mean that' and I think she is genuinely lonely.

'Everything OK?' asks Mum as I come back into the house. She's standing by the door and she gives a big sigh of relief. She's clearly been waiting for me, worrying. I made it. I went next door to deliver a parcel and came back again.

'Don't make a big deal of it, Mum,' I beg.

'It's progress, Kasia – progress,' Mum says softly.

I nod. I am mega pleased with myself, though I'd never admit it to Mum.

Back upstairs I rest in bed for a while and then go and sit by the window. A few people are walking along the pavement, each in their own separate world, though they are only metres apart. A man on his mobile, a woman with smart high-heeled boots, a teenage girl with a bobble hat. A silver car appears and slows down near the girl. There's something weirdly familiar about the scene, and my heart skips a beat as I remember the abduction. Is this the same car I saw? Is it going to happen again – to this girl? I am frozen to the spot.

The car pulls over, parks and a man gets out. He glances towards the girl. I hold my breath. She's still walking, she hasn't noticed the car. Fear rises in my throat – but the man is walking the other way.

He's heading for the barber's on the corner. He goes inside.

I look again at the silver car and realise it isn't the same kind. It's a three door and a completely different shape.

My eyes turn towards the upstairs window at the house opposite. The curtains are closed and there's no one there – but then I see one curtain move. A hand – a face – dark eyes, looking out. Then nothing. Again, I didn't see clearly, but I'm sure it's the same face I glimpsed before and I'm even more certain now that it wasn't the face of the woman who lives there. This face is narrower, younger. A girl. Who is she? She disappeared so quickly.

The couple have a baby, but I've never seen a girl come in or out of that house. If she's the one who was looking out of the window, then why did the woman lie about anyone else living there?

5

'Mum, did you know there's a girl living over at number forty-eight?' I ask. 'As well as that couple and their baby. 'I've never seen her go out. Don't you think that's weird?'

'A girl? I've not seen a girl,' Mum says as she picks up an empty mug from my bedside cabinet. 'Are you sure?'

'Yes,' I tell her.

I start watching the girl's window more closely. I'm certain she's real. A couple of days later, I see her again, just as I hear Mum coming up the stairs. I call her urgently. I want her to see the girl – to prove that she exists. Mum comes running, thinking something's wrong.

'Mum – look! She's there now! The girl!'

I only turned away for a second, but as Mum reaches the window and I turn back, the girl has gone.

Mum peers across the road. 'I don't see her,

mój kotku. What's so interesting about this girl?'

'I think it was her,' I tell Mum. 'I think she was the one who saw what I saw, when that woman was dragged into the car. And the police didn't speak to her, did they? Should I call the police again and tell them?'

'But the police went and talked to the people in the house, and nobody saw anything. You know that,' says Mum. 'If a woman *was* abducted, surely someone would have missed her by now and reported it. They found no one missing, did they? Maybe you mistook what you saw?'

I shake my head. 'I know what I saw – and there is a girl across the road. I've seen her too. And I never see her go out.'

'Someone could say the same about you,' Mum comments.

'Yes. Maybe that's it!' I exclaim. 'She could be ill like me – and that's why she doesn't go out. Perhaps the people across the road didn't want her stressed with questions and that's why they didn't mention her to the police?'

'It's possible, I suppose,' says Mum. 'If unlikely.'

'I want to go across the road and ask them,' I tell

Mum. 'Maybe we could even be friends?'

'Oh Kasia. I don't want you going round there annoying them. If you really think this girl exists and she might be stuck inside, ill like you, then perhaps I could go over and ask for you.'

'Would you, Mum? Thanks! That'd be great.'

Mum goes downstairs and I sit at the window and watch her cross the road to number forty-eight. It's the man who opens the door. I can see Mum talking, but she isn't there long.

I wait eagerly for her to come in and back upstairs.

'So?' I ask. 'What did he say?'

'Well, I asked – you saw me. And the man had no idea what I was talking about,' she tells me. 'I felt embarrassed, Kasia.'

'What did he say?'

Mum gives me a quizzical look. 'He said there's no girl there.'

'What? Did he speak English? Maybe he didn't understand,' I say, bewildered.

'He had an accent, but his English was clear enough,' says Mum. 'Perhaps you imagined her. Or maybe a girl *was* there and now she's gone – I don't know. But she isn't there now and I think you should put your mind to other things.'

I go and lie down on the bed – but I can't stop thinking about it. I don't understand what's going on. The man must be lying – but why would he? I'm sure I saw her! Only glimpses I know, but why would I imagine it? If only she wouldn't always vanish so quickly . . .

As I think more, prickles start running up my spine. And then I start having properly crazy thoughts, like, what if the reason she vanishes so quickly and that no one else has seen her, not even the people who live there – what if that's because she's . . . a ghost?

Today I looked out of the window — even though I know that I should not — and I was shocked. I saw the ghost of myself — looking back at me. A girl in the window opposite. She peered out, just as I did, her shadowy shape a mirror-image of mine, though her hair was light, her face pale. Is she a ghost, just as I am? Is the whole street perhaps full of ghosts like me, and we know nothing of each other's plight, or why we can neither live nor our souls rest in peace?

6

I look out of the window as often as I can that evening and the next day, but she doesn't reappear. Then, in the evening, I see the woman coming out of the house. She's on her mobile. She walks up past the bus stop towards the shops, barely glancing left or right as she crosses the road.

She's deep in conversation with someone and I can't help wondering what they're talking about. Perhaps she's telling a friend how the house gives her the creeps – especially that small front bedroom. She gets a chill every time she's in there and it makes her shudder. She wants to move.

I know this is just my imagination running riot but as I watch, the woman turns and walks back to the house, still speaking in an animated way into the phone. She isn't going anywhere – she just came out to talk privately. Maybe she was nervous of speaking about the weird atmosphere in that room. She can't tell her husband. He'd think she was crazy. And she can't explain it but she feels as if she's being watched.

She looks like she's shouting into the phone now. She's so loud I can hear a bit of it but I can't make out the words and anyway, I don't think it's English.

The woman is back at her front door now. She glances up in my direction as she takes a key from her pocket, and she sees me. I pull back from the window, embarrassed, partly about being seen amd partly because of the story I've been making up. I wait a minute and then look out cautiously again. She must have gone inside.

The ghost theory keeps going round and round in my head even though I try to ignore it. I don't think I believe in ghosts but right now I can't think of another reason why I keep seeing a girl that nobody else sees – not even the people who live there.

When I feel up to it, I ask Mum to bring me my tablet so I can do some research. I can't spend too long on it or I get headaches.

I start by looking up the address, forty-eight New Weald Road. Maybe I can find out who lives there, or even if anyone has ever died there. I don't expect to find anything, but at least I'm doing something.

The first Google entries are property pages, house prices and homes for rent and for sale. Then there are the shops, the hairdressers. There's a report on a burglary at number 249. A bus route being diverted. I keep scrolling through pages. It's very boring and my head soon starts to hurt, so I stop.

I lie down and decide to try meditating, which a doctor said might help me. Mum wasn't impressed with the suggestion, but I found I quite like it. I have an app on my phone and it is definitely relaxing and something I can do without effort. Mum is baking downstairs. The smell wafts up and I start by visualising a piece of cake in my mind, focusing on that and nothing else.

Thoughts keep drifting back, though, even as I try to let them go. Maybe I need to think of another way to research, like asking someone who knows the area. I wonder if Mrs Gayatri could help – she's lived here a long time.

'I was thinking I might go next door and visit Mrs Gayatri,' I tell Mum next time I'm well enough to be downstairs.

Mum glances up doubtfully. 'Are you up to it? And

I'm not sure you should go bothering her. I think she prefers her own company.'

'Maybe that's because she doesn't have any other option,' I suggest. 'Anyway, she invited me – when I took that parcel round. She sounded like she really wanted me to come.'

'OK, if you want to.' Mum smiles. 'Don't stay too long, though – you don't want to tire her, or yourself either. Here – I'll give you some apple cake to take with you.'

Like last time, Mrs Gayatri takes ages to come to the door.

'Another parcel?' she asks, looking puzzled. 'I don't remember ordering anything.'

'No, this is some of Mum's apple cake,' I tell her. 'I've come to visit, if that's OK? But say if you don't feel like company. I won't mind.'

'How lovely!' Mrs G smiles, her wrinkles briefly ironed out with pleasure. 'Come on in, dear. Do you mind taking your shoes off?'

Even though we've lived next door to Mrs Gayatri for ten years, I've never once stepped inside this house and it feels weird following Mrs G into the hallway. I take my shoes off and put them on the mat.

'I don't get many visitors,' she says, sighing as she leads me into a rather dark living room. She points to the red velvet armchair. 'Sit yourself down. Can I get you a tea or coffee? Will you help me eat this cake?'

While she makes the tea, I sit looking around the room. There's a slight smell of incense and a small statue in the corner that is part elephant, part man. There are photos – some very old sepia ones of people that look like they were taken in India. There's one black-and-white wedding photo and I wonder if it's Mrs Gayatri's own wedding picture. I go closer to look.

Mrs G comes back in with flowery teacups and saucers on a tray. She sets it down on a small, dark, wooden table and then goes back for the cake slices on two matching china plates.

'I was just looking at your pictures. I hope you don't mind,' I say.

'That was my wedding – so, so many years ago.' She smiles. 'My darling husband Vijay. He died ten years ago and I still miss him so much. These are my parents – they of course died many, many years ago – and my five big brothers too.'

'Do you have no other family – no children of

your own?' I ask.

Mrs G's mouth turns down, her eyes look suddenly glassy and I wish I hadn't asked.

'I'm so sorry – I didn't mean to upset you,' I say.

'It's fine,' she assures me. 'Just hard when everyone I love has gone.' She sighs again. 'Life must be hard for you too, being stuck at home so much.'

'At least I have my mum,' I say. 'She's had to give up her job to look after me, though. And Dad's working harder than ever.'

'Are you not going to school at all?'

'Not since last June,' I explain. 'I have a tutor who comes once a week. I have constant pain in my arms and legs and I just get so tired when I do anything. It's really frustrating. But I think I am improving now.'

'What is the cause?' she asks. 'Do they know why it started?'

I shake my head. 'I had tonsillitis and I just didn't get better. No one knows why it happens.'

'And is there treatment for it?'

'There's a bit of research going on, but they know so little about it, there isn't much on offer. I'm on a waiting list to see a consultant. The doctor just told me to try to pace myself.'

'But you will recover?'

'I hope so.'

There's silence for a moment. I don't want to think about my illness – about the possibility that I'll be like this forever. I change the subject.

'Mrs Gayatri, I wanted to ask you something,' I say now. 'I'm interested in the history of our street and I know you've lived here a long time. I wondered if you have any memories to share of anything that has happened here?'

'What kind of thing?' she asks.

'Any memorable events, things that shocked you, tragedies?'

'That's a strange question!' Mrs G shakes her head. 'Surely you are better to focus your energies on happier things. Let me think . . . now there's Amir and Zainab, of course, across the road. Their daughter died. That was most certainly a tragedy. She was so young. Their only child. That must have been twenty-five years ago. But that's probably not the sort of thing you mean. Now, what else . . .'

'The girl across the road – can you tell me any more?' I ask, leaning forward. 'What happened to her?'

Mrs G shakes her head. 'Really, it is upsetting for me even to think about it. Let's talk of happier things and leave the past behind. It will do your health no good to focus on such sadness. Shall I show you what came in that parcel the other day?'

I nod. I'm frustrated. I am desperate to know more but I don't want to push her if it's upsetting her. She walks slowly back into the kitchen and returns with a bird feeder.

'I love my garden but I'm not up to tending it like I used to,' she tells me. 'I like to watch the birds, though. I wondered, as you're here, whether you might do me a favour and hang it outside for me – on the silver birch. I have the seeds to fill it with. Then I can sit by the back window and watch for the birds. They'll be grateful now the weather's getting colder.'

This sounds sad to me – having nothing more interesting to do than watching birds, though maybe it is no sadder than watching the street like I do. I nod again and follow her to the back door, which she unlocks. The garden, which looked overgrown when I last glimpsed it from my parents' bedroom window, looks far wilder from down here. Neglect has turned it into a jungle.

'This garden was beautiful once,' Mrs G says wistfully. 'My husband and I – we were both keen gardeners. But now I don't have the strength for it, nor the money to pay a gardener.'

'I wish I could help,' I tell her, 'but I don't have the strength either.'

Actually, it's the last thing I'd want to do, even if I did have full strength. Gardening isn't my idea of fun at all.

'Of course you don't, my dear, but it's a kind thought.'

She seems so sad, I struggle for something positive to say. 'I guess it's good for wildlife?'

'True,' she says, but I sense this is little consolation.

I fill the feeder and find I can easily hang it on a branch. Mrs G's house is on the corner and it's the only one in our row that has a decent sized garden. I've never been very interested in gardens, but I do vaguely remember it being much neater in the past. I used to be envious as a young child because we only have a small paved back yard with no lawn or plants at all.

'Thank you so much!' she says. 'That's wonderful. I'd have to stand on a stool to do that and I knew it wasn't a good idea.'

'No, you mustn't go doing things like that,' I agree. 'It's nice to be able to do something helpful for a change. It's usually me who needs the help.'

'Well, I'm very grateful,' she says.

'I'd better go now,' I tell her. I suddenly feel so tired – and she is looking tired, too. She doesn't protest and I wonder if I have already outstayed my welcome.

'I hope you will come again,' she says. 'It's been so nice to have some company.'

I'm relieved. I was worried I'd upset her asking about tragedies, and that she wouldn't want me back. I'm glad I came, though – Mrs G did seem genuinely pleased to see me, and I even learned something about the girl over the road. At least, I may have done. I learned there was a tragedy, and it involved a girl who died. Does that mean the girl I see really is a ghost? I wish I knew the whole story.

7

'A gummy bear factory! My son is making gummy bears?'

Dad has somehow seen Mum's latest WhatsApp message from Marek, who has moved from sprinkling cheese on pizzas to making gummy bears. Dad is reeling off a torrent of Polish insults.

'Why my son? Why me? We bring him here for a good life, he has a good education and he throws it all away to make teddy bear sweets! What did I do to deserve this useless child?'

'Don't say that, Dad,' I protest. Dad has a tendency to be overdramatic, but to me this seems unfair.

'Sorry, *moje kochanie*, I don't want to upset you.' Dad gently strokes my hair. 'But gummy bears! *Pah!*'

A few days later I get a package from Germany. Marek has written a card saying how much he misses me and enclosed five packets of gummy bears. I wish he'd come home.

I have a bad day for no apparent reason. That's what it's like. I spend the morning in bed eating gummy bears and then the afternoon sitting up, looking out of the window. I've been looking out every day, but I haven't seen the girl again.

Mum is worrying that I'm seeing things – as in imagining them. I overheard her telling Dad. I get brain fog sometimes. I can't think straight and I struggle with the school work my tutor leaves for me, but hallucinations are not a symptom of ME. I know that because I looked it up online. Even so, the more I watch from the window and don't see the girl, the more I doubt my own memory. I'm wondering if I really saw her at all or if it was a trick of the light. It's easier to think of her as a ghost than as a real person – but if she was real, perhaps she was staying there and now she's gone. I hope so, but either way, I can't stop thinking about her. I wish I could.

It's almost a relief when my home tutor, Judy, gets here and I can think of something else. She sits on the wicker chair in my room, runs her hand through her thick dark hair and adjusts her big glasses as she checks my attempts at some maths problems. I'm panicking that I'm getting so far behind at school.

'I want you to give me more work, Judy,' I tell her. 'I'm not doing enough. How am I ever going to catch up?'

'You can only do what you can do,' she says. 'I don't want to give you too much. It will stress you out and that'll set you back further. But you're doing OK, and you *are* getting better. You couldn't have done maths like this a few weeks ago.'

'My head is less fuzzy,' I agree, 'but, Judy, I'm so far behind! I'm meant to be taking ten GCSEs. Even if I get back to school, how will I do it?

'Maybe you could cut down on the number of subjects? she suggests.

I shake my head. 'I don't want to give any up.'

'Or you could perhaps stay in Year 9, repeat the year.'

'Never,' I say emphatically. 'Can you imagine how awful that would be? I want to be with my friends.'

'Don't think about it now,' Judy tells me. 'Keep working like you are and get plenty of rest too. Just focus on one day at a time.'

It's easy for her to say but the thought of staying down a year, while my friends all do their GCSEs next year and then go into the sixth form without me, is more than I can bear. I won't let that happen. I have to get better and back to school as soon as possible. If Judy won't give me more work then I will get it from Ellie.

Once Judy's gone, I work hard on more maths, but I'm exhausted and I don't manage as much as I'd hoped. My eyes are drooping. I wish I had more energy and could concentrate better. But Judy has said that I'm improving. So that gives me hope.

The next day, Ellie is due to visit and this time I'm determined to remember to tell her about the girl, as I'm sure she'll be able to help me think it through. But when she arrives she's with Lia, and I'm not sure how I feel about it. Lia's in our form group but I don't know her that well. We've never been friends.

'You were moaning that no one else comes to see you, so I brought Lia,' Ellie tells me. 'We've been working together in drama. We've done this sketch – you really should see it. It's hilarious! We might even do it in the show next term!'

She exchanges glances with Lia and they both start giggling. They're clearly waiting for me to ask them to perform it for me. I feel a tingle of jealousy that they seem so close. I wonder if Lia's trying to replace me as Ellie's bestie – but I am also curious about this sketch.

'You going to show me then?' I ask.

'OK – with any luck a laugh will do you good and not tire you out,' Ellie says, grinning.

The sketch has me in stitches – I laugh so much that I ache. It may hurt physically but I do feel better inside.

'Do you think you'll be back at school soon?' Lia asks, when we can finally speak again.

I shrug. 'I hope so.'

'You must be so bored stuck in here,' she says. 'Or have you been doing some writing? That story you wrote was so brilliant – it's fab that you've won that competition!'

She sounds genuinely pleased for me and my feelings towards her soften.

'I don't really feel up to writing,' I tell her. 'I'm sure I will get back to it soon, though.'

'Lia and I are going to Dimitri's New Year's Eve party!' Ellie says.

'Dimitri's? But you can't stand him!'

'Oh – he's all right. Loads of people are going.'

'Could be fun, I guess.'

'Yeah, well, I'll tell you how it goes,' Ellie says, laughing.

'Who throws up where and when, you mean?' Lia giggles.

Ellie turns to me. 'Remember that time at Erin's party, Kas?' She grins. 'When you had to rescue me?'

'What happened?' asks Lia.

It takes a few seconds but the memory comes flooding back. 'Oh, yeah! You got locked in the loo!' I laugh.

'There was someone in the downstairs loo, so I had to go up,' Ellie tells Lia. 'Then the door wouldn't open and I was yelling and yelling – but the music was so loud no one heard me.'

'And I was dancing with Serene and Erin,' I say, 'and waiting for you, and you took ages, so in the end I came up to look for you and heard you shouting!'

'So how did you get out?' Lia asks.

'Erin found a screwdriver and undid the door handle,' I tell her.

'I'd have been stuck there for hours otherwise,' says Ellie. I thought I was going to have to climb out the tiny bathroom window and shimmy down the drainpipe!'

Now it's me and Ellie laughing together, and Lia's turn to join in.

After they leave, I feel glad that Lia came. Ellie will always be my best friend, but it was nice to talk to someone else for a change.

I turn my chair back to the window and sit looking out. It's weird, thinking back to Erin's party – dancing and laughing with my friends, having fun. It's like that was another lifetime. But I will get better – I am determined to get back to these things. I see movement in the corner of my eye but when I look there's nothing. Did the curtain move? Was she there, and did she fade away instantly, as always? I wanted to wave – to let her know I'm here. Perhaps she'd stay visible if she knew someone could see her.

I need to find out more. I don't want to upset Mrs G, but right now she's the only one who can help. I need to talk to her again.

I've knocked on the door and I'm waiting and waiting for Mrs Gayatri to come and answer it.

She looks surprised. 'How are you, dear?' she asks. 'What can I do for you?'

'I thought I'd come for a chat, but only if it's

convenient,' I say.

She smiles and holds the door for me.

'I'm so glad you came again,' she says. 'Those hungry birds have got through all the food already. I've seen blue tits there, and great tits. If you could refill the bird feeder for me I'd be so pleased.'

'Of course,' I tell her.

'You do that while I make some tea.'

When I've refilled the feeder, we sit on armchairs opposite each other.

'Mrs Gayatri, you know you told me about the girl who died across the road? I don't want to upset you, but I'd really like to know more about what happened.'

She frowns. 'To lose your only child – it's such a sad thing,' she says quietly. 'She was a sweet girl. Meningitis, it was. There's nothing more to tell really.'

'Meningitis?' I repeat. 'So she was ill?'

I was expecting something more dramatic – something that would give a reason for her to be appearing as a ghost.

Mrs G nods. 'Nasty illness that – can still be a killer, even now. Her parents moved away in the end. I think it was hard for them to see . . .' She pauses, her eyes glassy for a moment. 'To see other children growing up in the street when their child was no longer there. It was empty for over a year after they went, number forty-six. I think people viewing the house could still sense the sadness.'

'You mean forty-eight?' I ask.

'Forty-eight? No.' Mrs G frowns. 'What makes you say that? It was forty-six.'

'Forty-six?' I stare at her in surprise. 'Are you sure?'

'Yes.' She nods firmly. 'Poor Shari, she was only five, you know.'

I am speechless, silent, as I try to take this in. This isn't about my girl at all – it's the wrong house, and the girl is the wrong age. So now I'm back to knowing nothing at all!

Mrs G looks so sad. I know it was a tragic thing, but I'm surprised that she is this upset.

'I'm so sorry I asked you about it,' I tell her. 'I didn't mean to upset you.'

'Never mind,' she says. 'Let's say no more about it.'

8

It's Christmas Eve. We were supposed to be in Poland having a big family celebration, like last year. My cousin Aleksandra and I had such a great time together walking round the Christmas markets, so pretty in the crisp, white snow, and then back to my aunt and uncle's for delicious hot chocolate. Christmas in Lodz is like the pictures you get in England on Christmas cards, but I've never actually seen snow in England at Christmas. I like living here but I love spending Christmas in Poland and I especially love the buzz of being part of a much larger family – that's something I never feel here in England.

But we're not there because I'm not up to the long journey, and I feel so bad about it. Mum is trying to put on a brave face. Dad is taking the chance to do a bit of DIY – fixing a cupboard door that never shuts, and putting up a new shelf in the kitchen. The banging is giving me a headache and I'm relieved when it stops.

Then it's too quiet – especially without Marek.

I've been hoping desperately that he might come home for Christmas, that he'll just turn up and surprise us. We've never had a Christmas without the four of us being together. He's not been in touch. Even as the fish is cooking for our traditional Christmas Eve meal, there's a sound outside and Mum rushes to the front door, but it was only someone putting through leaflets.

We eat our Christmas Eve meal – twelve dishes including fried fish and potatoes – and Mum goes to church for Midnight Mass and then again on Christmas morning. Dad stays with me. He's never been so keen on church. He finds YouTube clips of funny kittens attacking Christmas trees to show me, trying to cheer us both up.

'I'm so sorry, Dad,' I tell him.

'What you have to be sorry for?' he asks gently.

'I know you love Christmas in Poland with Uncle Andrzej and Auntie Maria as much as Mum does. It's all my fault.'

'My lovely girl, we'll soon have you well. We will be in Poland again – maybe in the summer.'

'I hope so, Dad.'

Mum is trying so hard. She's made her special Christmas cake. We have an amazing tree. But where's Marek? He's not been in touch. He hasn't even responded to my messages.

The radio and TV give the impression of fun but there are no cousins chattering and laughing, no aunt and uncle bickering, which makes me think of Mrs Gayatri. It must be like this for her all the time.

'I'm feeling bad that Mrs Gayatri is on her own,' I say to Mum. 'Maybe we could ask her in for Christmas dinner later?'

We had our main meal last night, but we like to adopt some English traditions too and are having turkey for Christmas day.

Mum hesitates. 'I'm not sure, love. She's a Hindu. I don't think she'll want to celebrate Christmas.'

'But she's all alone,' I say, frowning.

Mum meets my eyes, smiling softly. 'There's no harm in asking her, if you want to.'

I go next door, knock and wait.

'Happy Christmas!' Mrs G says as she opens it. 'I didn't expect to see you today. Aren't you busy celebrating?'

'We usually go to Poland,' I tell her, 'but I'm not

well enough to travel. We wondered if you'd like to join us for dinner. Unless it's against your religion?'

'How kind! I don't celebrate Christmas, but I would be glad of company today – if you're sure. Oh, but I am vegetarian. Is that a problem? I could always eat before I come . . .'

'It won't be a problem,' I say, hoping that's true.

'That is very kind – please tell your parents not to go to any trouble. What time would you like me?'

'3 p.m.'

'I will see you then.' Mrs G smiles warmly. 'Thank you for thinking of me, Kasia.'

I feel good as I go back home and tell Mum that Mrs G has said yes. 'Mum, she seemed really pleased to be asked.'

'Well, there's plenty of food!' Mum smiles.

'Actually she's vegetarian,' I announce.

'Oh.' Mum frowns. 'What shall I do? She can't just eat potatoes and Brussels sprouts!'

I shrug. 'I'm sure she doesn't mind what she eats, as long as it isn't meat. She was just happy to be invited.'

'She probably only likes spicy food anyway,' says Mum, tutting. She opens the cupboard where she keeps herbs and spices and starts rummaging. 'I don't have many Indian spices, but I'll see what I can do. Oh, Kasia – I feel awful. I know you're trying to be kind but it will be so embarrassing.'

'Please don't worry, Mum,' I tell her, and now I feel guilty for stressing her out when I'm not even up to helping with the cooking.

Dad makes a face when I say Mrs G is coming. 'I was going to have a nice sleep in front of the TV. Now I'll have to dress up?' he asks.

'Not dress up – just dress, Dad,' I tell him. Dad is still in his pyjamas.

It's his turn to tut. 'And what will we talk about? We have nothing in common.'

I'm beginning to feel a bit stressed myself now, so I go and lie down on the sofa. To my surprise I go to sleep and when I wake up, Mum is poking something in my face.

Here, Kasia – taste this,' Mum says, holding out a spoon of brownish mush. 'It's a curried lentil dish. I didn't have all of the ingredients, so I don't know if it's all right or not.'

I taste the food, and I'm about to tell her it's fine when suddenly it feels like my mouth is on fire! I rush for a glass of water, but it's ages before I can speak.

'Oh, Mum! How much chilli did you put in that?' I ask, my eyes streaming.

'I'm not sure,' she says. 'So – no good then?' She takes a taste too.

We look at each other – and then suddenly we're both laughing. Mum's usually so good at cooking, but this is really terrible.

Dad comes and looks at us, laughing and crying together, and backs off hastily, muttering in Polish.

'Oh dear,' Mum says when she can talk again. 'I'm running out of time. I'll make a salad too – that will have to do.'

When Mrs G arrives, she brings a large plastic bowl with a lid. 'I couldn't expect you to cook specially for me,' she says, 'so I've made a dish with chickpeas and vegetables which we can all share.'

'It smells wonderful,' says Mum, smiling.

Mrs G's dish is full of flavour, but it isn't spicy-hot at all. Even Dad tries some of it and declares it delicious. 'Complements the turkey perfectly,' he tells Mrs G, who beams back at him, delighted.

We talk about the snowy Christmases in Poland, and Mrs G tells us about her first experience of snow when she came to this country in 1974. Mum then tells her about when we moved to the UK.

'We came in 2005 – the economy was so bad in Poland. Stefan realised that he could earn as much here in one week, no – one day, as he could earn in a month in Lodz.'

'That's why you came?' Mrs G asks.

'Yes – we thought we were coming to paradise, you know? We found an amazing house on the internet and the price looked so good. It was near Manor House and Seven Sisters. Then we arrived and discovered we were paying for one room only. There were twenty other people sharing the house! It was such a shock. Later, we met kinder people, though – people who helped us.'

Mum and Dad ask Mrs G about her life and family but she gives short answers and quickly turns the conversation back to us. Dad starts telling us jokes and some even make Mrs G laugh out loud. She surprises us by telling a few good ones herself. Then Dad does his party piece of making his ears waggle. His face goes bright red when he does it and his eyes look like they're popping out.

'Well, in all my years, I have never met anyone who can do that!' Mrs G chuckles. 'I am having the loveliest time. Thank you so much.'

'And now please join us in our special after dinner ceremony!' Dad announces.

Mrs G looks slightly worried.

'What ceremony?' I demand.

'The "let's sit in the lounge and watch TV" ceremony,' Dad says, waving his arms in a triumphant gesture.

Mrs G smiles with relief.

'Are you up to watching a little, my *kotku*?' Dad asks me.

I've been having a lovely day but now I realise I need a rest. The glands in my neck have started throbbing and my legs feel achey. I can't cope with watching TV, but I lie on the sofa with my eyes shut while the others all watch a film. I am so happy we invited Mrs G – they are all getting on so well.

Afterwards we play charades. I'm not up to performing but guess some of the answers. I laugh so hard at Dad's James Bond impression that my throat hurts. I'm feeling happy though, when I excuse myself and go upstairs to bed.

9

I'm sitting in the kitchen with Mum, eating freshly baked orange and almond cake. It's one of my grandmother's recipes that Mum is trying to recreate from memory. She's always wishing she had the old family recipe book, but that got left behind in Poland. I'm lucky that I don't gain weight easily, even though I'm not exercising much – but still, I am trying not to eat too much cake.

'It's not like my mother's. What do you think, Kasia?'

'It's so good!' I moan.

It's a big one – I'll have to freeze most of it,' Mum tells me.

'Shall I take some to Mrs Gayatri?' I ask.

'What a nice idea,' says Mum. 'I think she enjoyed Christmas with us, didn't she?'

She cuts a large slice of cake and wraps it in foil, while I put my coat on. It's the middle of January and getting colder every day and dark so early too. I tap the knocker. I wait, knowing that as usual she may take some time. Perhaps it's just the cold, but I feel as if I've been waiting longer than usual. I knock again. There's still no answer. Maybe Mrs G is out on one of her rare visits to the shops. I turn to go back home but something stops me. What if she is there, but she's unwell or something? I tap the knocker harder. Then I lift the letterbox flap and call through.

'Mrs Gayatri! It's Kasia.'

No answer. I try to look through the letterbox. There's a guard with well-worn bristles and it isn't easy to see through, but I'm sure there's a dark shape on the floor at the end of the hallway by the kitchen.

'Mrs Gayatri! It's Kasia. Are you OK?'

As my eyes adjust to the gloom, I make out a shoe shape. A shoe and part of a leg. I gasp. It's her! She's lying there on the floor, not moving . . . not moving at all.

I try the side gate but it's locked so I come back to the front. I put the cake down on the doorstep and keep calling her through the letterbox, at the same time reaching into my coat pocket for my phone. My hand is shaking and I can hardly get a grip on it.

I call 999.

'Ambulance please!' My voice comes out squeaky, not like my normal voice at all. 'It's my neighbour. She's lying on the floor in her hallway and she's not moving. I can see her through her letterbox. It's forty-seven New Weald Road.'

They ask me questions that I wish I could answer with 'yes'. Can I get in? Do I know where she keeps a spare key? Do I have a contact number for a family member?

I check under the doormat and in the flowerpots by the front door but I can't find a key. There's a small inauspicious pile of rocks on the other side of the door and half-heartedly I lift those too and reveal two keys.

I look down the road, hoping the ambulance will appear and I'll be able to hand the keys over without going in myself. Should I call Mum? No, I have to go in. I fiddle with the keys, my hands still shaking and the door clicks open.

I hesitate – scared, scared to go closer. Maybe Mrs G is dead and I don't want to see her close up if she is. I can imagine her eyes – glassy and scary like in films. If she is dead should I close them? I've seen that in films too but I don't want to touch a dead person.

Mrs Gayatri is lying crumpled, her feet sticking out at an awkward angle through the doorway to the kitchen. I can't see her head. I edge nearer, on tiptoes for some reason, as if any sound might wake her – but I want her to wake up. I want it more than anything.

'Mrs Gayatri?' I call.

I bend over her. She seems to jerk slightly. Her head is on one side. There's blood, a gash on the side of her head and a pool of blood underneath. I gulp. Nausea rises in my throat. It looks as if someone has hit her hard on the head. Did someone attack her? Something is sparkling on the floor beside her. Fragments of glass. Did someone hit her over the head with a bottle or a vase? Then I see a dark wooden photo frame on the floor. Someone must have hit her and she fell against the wall, knocking the picture off its hook.

My heart is pounding. Taking care not to tread on the glass, I crouch and put my hand under Mrs G's nose. To my relief I feel air moving. She is definitely breathing.

'Mrs Gayatri! Mrs Gayatri!' I call. 'It's Kasia from next door. Don't worry – an ambulance is coming.'

A small sound comes from her, but it isn't words. I wait. It feels like forever. I feel so alone, with such a huge responsibility – someone's life and there's nothing I can do except crouch here and hold her hand.

I wonder what Mum would do and then I phone her. She says she'll come straight away. I've got this weird floaty feeling in my stomach, like the lava lamp someone bought me. I glance down at the photo frame, The picture, which I think is of Mrs G's husband when he was young, has slipped out and there is another photo behind. I see it is a picture of Mr and Mrs G with a girl around my age standing in-between them, smiling straight at the camera.

Before I have time to wonder about this girl, Mum has arrived and has her arms round my shoulder, and the ambulance is here too, with two paramedics.

'You're her neighbour? Perhaps you could give us a few details,' the woman paramedic asks Mum. 'What is her full name, date of birth? Do you know her next of kin?'

Mum can only give Mrs G's last name. She never told us her first name or her birthday, and she has no family that we knew of.

The paramedic turns to me. 'Kasia, is it? You're the one who called us? You did the right thing.'

'You should call the police,' I tell her. 'I think she was attacked – see that gash on her head?'

'You saw someone attack her?' she asks, looking alarmed.

'No, no.' I shake my head. This is so awful.

'Looks like a stroke to me,' I hear the woman paramedic say. 'She must have hit her head on the wall as she fell. That's why it's bleeding. There's no sign of an attack, is there?' she asks the male paramedic who is examining Mrs G.

'No,' comes the answer.

'But . . . the gash . . .' I say. 'I thought . . . the blood . . .' I can feel my cheeks flushing red with embarrassment.

'She has a big imagination,' I hear Mum say quietly, embarrassing me even more.

'Mum...'

'You did a good thing,' Mum says to me now, squeezing my shoulders. 'My Kasia, you're a good, brave girl.'

As Mrs Gayatri is carried out on a stretcher, I realise I still have the photo in my hand. Who is the girl standing in the middle and why was this picture hidden behind another? I stare at it for a moment, then tuck the photo under my coat.

I turn towards the ambulance. 'Do you think she'll be OK?' I ask the woman paramedic.

'She's in the best hands now,' she replies.

The doors slam and the ambulance disappears down the road.

Mum squeezes my hand. 'So sad,' she says, 'to see her like that.'

'You don't think she's going to die, do you?' I ask.

'I hope not,' says Mum. 'I offered to go with her in the ambulance, but they said no.'

'I think I need to lie down,' I tell her, as exhaustion suddenly overtakes me.

'I'm not surprised – what a shocking thing!' says Mum. 'Thank goodness you found her, that's all I can say, or who knows how much longer she could have been lying there. I'll call the hospital later, and maybe go and visit her tomorrow.'

When Dad comes home we tell him all about it.

'I do feel sorry for the woman, not having family around her,' says Dad. 'But try not to get too involved, eh?' He gives Mum a hug.

Later, I lie in bed looking at the photo. Mrs G looks much younger but the girl couldn't be her daughter, could she? Mrs G would have mentioned her when I asked if she had any children. I think back, trying to remember her exact words. '*It's sad when everyone you love has gone.*' It was something like that.

The way the girl is standing between Mr and Mrs Gayatri — it definitely looks like a daughter with her parents. Unless she was a visitor — a niece or something. Perhaps Mrs G did have a daughter and she died — like the girl at number forty-six. But why then would she cover her photo? Surely she'd want to remember her.

I put the photo in my bottom drawer with the daffodil card that Josh signed, planning to give it back when Mrs G is home.

Mum calls the hospital to find out how Mrs G is, but as she's not family they are reluctant to tell her anything. Eventually they tell her that Mrs G definitely had a stroke, but that she's doing OK.

The next day Mum says she's going to visit her. I wish I could go too, but I am not well enough. I feel wiped out.

'Mum, before you go, take a look at this,' I say. I get the photo out of the drawer and tell her how I found it behind the picture in the smashed frame.

'Why did you take it?' Mum asks, frowning as she looks at it closely. 'You should have left it where you found it.'

'Mum – don't you think it looks like Mrs G had a daughter? The way she's standing between them?'

'Maybe,' says Mum, nodding.

'Why would she hide the picture away and say she has no family?' I ask.

'I don't know Kasia, I really don't.'

'Perhaps you should take the picture with you to the hospital,' I tell her. 'They wanted to know her next of kin, didn't they? Maybe show them.'

'Yes,' says Mum, though she looks a little hesitant. 'I don't want to interfere but I guess it doesn't do any harm to take it.'

When Mum's gone, I struggle out of bed and sit by the window. I look at the house opposite mine and I think about the face I saw – the girl. I wish she'd appear now, but she doesn't.

I'm lying down again when Mum comes back. I hear her feet hurrying up the stairs, faster than usual for Mum.

'Is Mrs G OK?' I ask, suddenly worried.

'Yes, she's improving,' Mum says, sitting on the edge of my bed. 'She's able to talk, though her words are a bit slurred. She was really pleased to see me. The nurses were pleased she had a visitor too as no one else has been and they said there's no next of kin to call on. So then I got out the photo.'

'Really? What happened?' I ask eagerly. I pull myself into a partial sitting position and Mum plumps up my pillow.

'We showed her the photo,' Mum tells me. 'I felt very awkward – I thought Mrs G was going to get angry, but she had tears in her eyes. She admitted that the girl is her daughter. Can you believe it?'

'Why has she kept her secret?' I ask. 'Why did she hide the photo?'

'Apparently they haven't spoken for fifteen years,' says Mum. 'Mrs G said she has no idea where she is now.'

'So they might not be able to find her?' I ask.

'They're going to try,' Mum tells me. 'Mrs G gave them her daughter's full name and date of birth, so we'll have to wait and see. If they find her, I only hope the daughter wants to see her mum. It's going to be very upsetting for Mrs G if not.'

'It's so sad that they fell out,' I say. 'Did she say why?'

'No,' Mum tells me.

'You should have asked,' I say.

'It's none of our business, Kasia,' says Mum. 'She'll tell us if she wants us to know.'

I know what Mum's saying, but I'm frustrated. For a mother and daughter not to speak for fifteen years, it must have been something big.

Later I get up again and sit at the window looking out. There's no sign of the girl across the road. There's an old woman at the bus stop. Her shopping bag is bulging and she leans it against the bench. She's looking at the timetable now but the bag is off balance and as I'm watching, it tips. A lemon falls out, followed by a packet of biscuits.

There's a boy walking past and he sees what's happened and stops. I gasp a little when I realise it's Josh. I haven't seen him for so long – he looks taller and his hair is longer. He crouches down and helps to gather the things. What a lovely thing to do. The woman thanks him profusely. I've seen her there before, and it's clear from her expression that she's not got much time for teenagers – thinks they are trouble with their rowdy music and mobile phones – so Josh has taken her by surprise with his kindness.

The old woman sits on the bench and tries once more to balance the bag, this time against one leg as she sits, with the other leg supporting it too. Hopefully it won't fall now. She watches Josh walk away – and so do I, longingly.

I wish I could call him. I wish he'd look up at the window and see me, but he doesn't. I watch him walk away until I can't see him any more.

10

I'm sitting at the kitchen table, drinking a herbal tea mix called 'Energy' while Mum's cooking chicken soup. This January weather is still so cold and gloomy we need it to warm us up. Steam rises from the stove.

'It's only two weeks until the award ceremony,' I remind Mum. 'I'm so excited about it.'

'Yes – I want to talk to you about that,' Mum says.

I look up to meet her eyes. Her serious expression makes me anxious.

'Is it Dad – can't he come?' I ask.

'He won't know until the last minute, Kasia. It isn't that.'

'What, then?'

Mum sighs as she breaks noodles into the soup. 'I'm so glad you're doing much better – coming downstairs, going next door,' she says, 'but it will be a long day and I'm worried it'll be too exhausting for you.'

I look at her in horror. 'I have to go, Mum. I must! It's the only thing I've been looking forward to.'

'I do want you to go,' Mum tells me. 'I just don't want you to undo all the progress you've made. There's so much to think about – there might be a lot of standing, and we might not be able stop the car near the theatre, so there will be walking too.'

'But Mum!' I glare at her fiercely.

'Let me finish, Kasia.' Mum holds up a hand to stop me. 'I've been making enquiries and I've found out we can get a wheelchair on loan. What do you think about that?'

'A wheelchair?'

This isn't what I was expecting. I feel all mixed up – relief that this isn't a fight about not going, but also a sadness and bitterness. Am I really so ill that I need a wheelchair? It feels like a backwards step.

'It will be less tiring for you,' Mum says.

'I hope you're not saying I should start using one all the time?' I ask.

'No, of course not. Just for this one occasion – and maybe other times to do things that would otherwise be too much. Let's just try it – that's all I'm saying.'

The idea of not having to walk, not having to stand,

definitely makes the whole outing feel more doable.

'OK,' I tell her. 'Just this once.'

When the wheelchair arrives Mum wants me to sit in it and try it straight away.

'I will be a learner driver, I need to practise!' she says.

I wish I could push myself but my arms aren't strong enough and this wheelchair is the kind with small wheels that's made to be pushed.

'I don't feel like it right now,' I say, though really I'm not keen on the looks I'll get from people we pass in the street – pitying looks.

'We need to try it some time,' says Mum – but she doesn't mention it again until a few days later when she says, 'Do you feel up to coming with me to visit Mrs Gayatri? I'm sure she'd be pleased to see you.' Then she adds tentatively, 'I thought it would be a chance to try out the wheelchair.'

I am still not keen on the wheelchair idea but I'd rather try it out in a hospital than along our street, and I would like to visit Mrs G.

'Just make sure you can push it without tipping me out face down,' I tease Mum. 'Although, at least there'd be doctors on hand if that happened!'

She laughs.

I haven't been in a car for months. The seatbelt is uncomfortable and I feel giddy as the car pulls away. I look out of the window and try to pretend I'm OK.

When we reach the hospital, Mum struggles to lift the wheelchair out of the car and get it open. I wait patiently in the passenger seat, wishing I could help. At last, I'm in the chair and she wheels me up the ramp into the building and down a series of long corridors. Mum's having no trouble pushing me and no one gives us a second glance. It feels weird but OK and I am relieved not to have to walk all this way.

Mrs Gayatri smiles a slightly lopsided but clearly happy smile as we arrive.

'Good idea,' she comments, 'using a wheelchair until you get your strength up. It's so nice of you to come and see me. And your mother was telling me you have your writing award ceremony soon!' she says. 'I will look forward to hearing all about it.'

I nod. 'I can't wait!'

Mum pulls up a chair and I stand up and move on to it while she parks the wheelchair in the corner.

'How are you?' I ask Mrs G. 'Are you going home soon?'

'In two or three days' time, they tell me,' she says. 'And I have some wonderful news!'

'Your daughter?' I ask, eagerly. 'Have they found her?'

'Yes! Oh, Kasia, I didn't think she would want to see me. She hasn't been in touch in all these years. But they contacted her and she is coming! I wish it hadn't taken something like this, but still, I cannot wait to see her – and I have a grandson too! They are coming to visit tomorrow.'

'Wow!' I say.

She reaches out a hand and I offer mine, which she squeezes gently. 'And it is thanks to you,' she says more quietly. 'It is thanks to you that I am alive and also that I will see Devi again, and meet my grandson. That photo . . . I couldn't understand where it had come from, but your mother explained about the broken frame.'

'Can I ask . . .' I begin, eager to know more, but I see Mum shaking her head sternly and I stop.

'Ask what, my dear?' says Mrs G.

'Oh . . . just . . . errr . . . how are you going to manage back at home on your own?'

'The hospital have told me they will send in people

to help me every day. Oh, I will be so glad to be back in my own home.'

'And I'll come in to visit more often,' I tell her.

'That will be lovely,' she says, nodding.

'And if you need anything, you must ask us,' adds Mum.

11

Next time Ellie comes to visit she brings Lia again. They are sitting cross-legged next to each other on my bed while I sit on the wicker chair.

'I've brought you some homework, like you asked,' Ellie says, handing me a pile of papers. 'But I have no idea why you want this stuff when you don't have to do it.'

'I've got to do it or I'll never catch up,' I tell her.

'Well, if there's anything you don't understand, just ask me,' says Ellie. 'But don't knock yourself out trying to do too much.'

'You sound like my mum – and Judy,' I say, smiling.

Ellie shrugs. 'I just want you to get better, so you can get back to school – oh – and so you can come to parties like Dimitri's and Tilly's party last week too!'

'How was it?' I ask.

'Actually it wasn't that great,' says Ellie.

'What happened?' I ask. 'Anyone there you liked?'

'It's all about getting off with someone,' she moans. 'That's all anyone seems to care about – and if you're not interested they just think you're playing hard to get. I had two boys almost fighting over me at one point, when I'd already told them both to get lost. Erin ended up with Kai, though.'

'How about you?' I ask Lia. She blushes and just shakes her head.

'So it wasn't much fun?' I ask.

Lia and Ellie exchange a quick glance as if sharing a private joke. I feel left out – they are becoming best friends, I can see it.

'Dimitri's party was better,' says Lia, turning back to me. 'He was so funny – he was acting totally wasted, like he could hardly stand up, but it turned out he was only pretending and he hadn't had a drop.'

'Why would he do that?' I laugh.

'I think he wanted to stay sober to make sure no one wrecked his parents' place.' She laughs too, and Ellie joins in.

They don't seem to have anything else to tell me, so I tell them about Mrs G's stroke.

'You probably saved her life,' Lia says, clearly impressed. 'It must have been so scary. It makes me think I should do a first aid course.'

'I went to see her in hospital,' I tell them.

'And you managed that OK?' says Ellie. 'Does that mean you're well enough to go the awards ceremony? It's next week, isn't it?'

I nod. 'I hope so. Mum's hired me a wheelchair.'

They both look a bit shocked at this and I wish I hadn't said it.

'Miss Giles is coming too.'

'Really? That's nice. Did you know that she's helping with the end of term show? She's been great. Look, I'm sorry I've not been to see you so much,' Ellie says. 'We're rehearsing and my mum's stressing out because she thinks I should be spending more time studying. She didn't want me to do the show in the first place but I convinced her I could do it and study. Now I'm not so sure. I didn't realise there would be quite so many rehearsals. Lia is so good in it! I hope you can come and see it, Kasia.'

'I'll see how I get on at the awards,' I tell her. 'If I manage that OK, maybe I can come to the show.'

'I'll keep my fingers crossed,' says Ellie. 'I'd love you to be there.'

Last year I was there – not in the audience but in

the orchestra for the first time. Our school has really good music and drama departments and they put on a show every Easter. Although I was nervous, it was amazing being part of it. I was looking forward to doing it again this year but now I will be lucky if I am well enough to watch.

Dad still doesn't know if he'll be able to get time off for the award ceremony but Miss Giles has offered to take us as Mum is worried about driving in central London. I am so excited, but also scared that I won't feel well enough on the day. I stay upstairs for a few days before the event, hoping to conserve my energy, but I can't help being anxious and I know that makes me worse.

On the day, I am relieved to find I don't feel too bad. Miss Giles also seems really excited when she comes to pick us up.

'I've entered students before for this award,' she tells me, 'but I've never had anyone win! They get thousands of entries from all over the country, you know. Most people will have travelled much further than us. There are categories for different age groups and genres, so with family members too I think there will be over a hundred people there.'

When we arrive Miss Giles drops us off as near to the theatre as she can and goes to park the car. She says she'll catch up with us inside. Mum pushes me the rest of the way in the wheelchair. It feels weird being pushed by Mum along the street – much weirder than in the hospital. I feel like a toddler in a buggy, as if I've grown down instead of up. We reach a road we need to cross and the wheelchair jerks on the big kerb, tipping me so I nearly fall out.

'Mum!' I yell.

'I'm so sorry – I'm not used to this,' she says. 'We should have practised more outside. The pavement isn't flat and easy, like in the hospital.'

I hate feeling so dependent and powerless. 'I'm getting out,' I tell her, standing up. 'Just to cross the road.'

It must look very odd to anyone passing, to see me stand up, walk quickly across the road and then sit down in the wheelchair again.

At last we reach the theatre, where I am welcomed like a celebrity. There's even a long red carpet, and everyone makes me feel very special.

'We have a ramp so you'll be able to get on to the

stage,' a woman tells me.

'It's OK – I can walk, just not very far,' I explain. Again, I know it will look weird to all these people here who've seen me in this wheelchair. They'll think I'm a fraud but I don't really care.

I am invited to sit on a chair on the stage while an actor reads the opening of my story. Listening to it, I feel an urge to start writing again. The applause is thrilling and as I look out into the audience I see that Dad is now sitting beside Mum and Miss Giles with the biggest grin on his face. I'm so happy he made it! When I'm given a glass trophy with my name engraved on it, I can even believe I'll be a real author one day.

The buzz of excitement has kept me going, but when it's all over and Dad wheels me back to our car I feel suddenly exhausted.

'Well done, Kasia!' says Miss Giles. 'I hope you will be back at school soon.'

'So do I,' I tell her.

'I am so proud of you, *moje kochanie*!' Dad says. 'We must go for a meal to celebrate. Maybe you will join us, Miss Giles?'

'That's kind of you to ask me, but I'll be off now,'

says Miss Giles. 'I have lots of marking to do. And Kasia does look tired.'

Mum shakes her head. 'A takeaway at home,' she suggests. 'Look at her.'

I agree – there's no way I could sit in a restaurant right now and by the time we get home I am not up to a takeaway either. I just want to go to bed and am relieved to make it up the stairs. It was worth it, though – it has been one of the best days of my life.

'Shall I do your curtains?' Mum offers, but I'm already halfway there.

'It's OK, Mum.'

'This is a day I will never forget,' she tells me, and I turn to meet her tired but smiling eyes. 'Such an achievement!'

'It was good to get out of here – to do something so special, Mum. And I will get better. I know I will.'

'You will,' she tells me. 'Sleep well, *mój aniele*.'

I turn to pull the curtain closed as Mum's footsteps tread the stairs. And I stop. She's there. The girl is there in the window. It's as if she's been waiting for me. She's staring straight at me – she's seen me, I'm sure. She looks solid – real – and she isn't vanishing. She looks so sad I feel a pang of guilt for having been out, having had such a lovely day. Then the curtains close across the road and she disappears from view.

We are finally connected – the girl looking through her window and me through mine, even though we know nothing about each other. I lie in bed, sure now that she's no ghost. She's real. So what's going on? Why did the man and woman who live in the house say there is no girl there? And why does she never come out?

12

When I wake up next morning, I feel a tingle of excitement that's not just left over from the awards. I'm still tired, but I am surprised and relieved that I don't feel too bad at all. In fact, I'm almost energetic! I feel determined to find out about the girl, and this time I'm not asking Mum – I'm going to go over to number forty-eight myself.

It's colder than yesterday and the chill wind hits me as I come out of the front door, almost as if it's trying to warn me off. I pull my coat tight around me as I stand on the kerb, checking for traffic before hurrying across. There's something reassuringly normal about walking out of the house and across the road, rather than being in a wheelchair like yesterday. I pause nervously outside the door but my legs are starting to ache so I ring the bell. I hold my breath as I wait, listening. I hear the sound of a baby crying and it's coming nearer. I breathe out, trying to remember what I planned to say.

The woman opens the door and stands in the doorway with a chubby, wailing baby, about six months old, in her arms.

'Hi,' I say awkwardly. 'I live across the road.'

'Oh, yes,' she says. 'Can I help you?' Her voice is not unfriendly, but there's something cagey about her expression. She shivers. 'I don't want to stand here long – he's not too happy as you can see – and I don't want him catching cold.' Her accent is strong, but her English clear. She squeezes the baby and he wriggles and cries louder, like he's trying to escape.

'I . . . I just wondered . . .' I have to speak loudly to be heard over the baby's cries. 'Is there a girl living here? Is she ill? I thought I saw her. I've been stuck at home – I'm not too well. I can't go to school and I don't see many people. I just wondered if she'd maybe . . . like to meet up, maybe we could get to know each other? I've noticed she doesn't seem to go out. I wondered if she might be ill, like me, and it would be weird if the two of us are stuck inside being ill but living opposite each other, if you know what I mean?'

I know I'm babbling and my legs are now throbbing.

The woman's eyebrows have gone up. 'Girl? Oh, you mean our niece? She's eighteen – not a girl like you. And she's not ill. She's staying with us and helping with the baby.'

'But she doesn't go out?' I query.

The woman shrugs. 'Not so often – she's a shy girl, prefers to stay at home. That is her choice. She's not in need of company. Is there anything else?'

'No. Sorry to bother you,' I tell her. The front door quickly closes. I hurry back into the warmth of my own house and sit on the sofa. I don't even have the strength to take off my coat.

The girl exists. Finally, someone else has acknowledged her existence. Was she upstairs watching when I saw that young woman dragged into the car? I replay the scene in my mind, wondering what happened next, where they took her, where she is now – and whether she's OK. That girl is the only one who could verify what I saw. If only I could talk to her.

Two days later, I am bedbound again. The delayed reaction is so hard to understand and it's like a kick in the teeth. It almost feels worse this time, because

I used the wheelchair to help me on the day, but it hasn't stopped this happening. It isn't fair.

I lie in bed thinking about the girl. When I stood there, at the door of number forty-eight, I believed the woman was telling me the truth, but now I am starting to feel suspicious again. I feel like something's wrong in that house, though I can't really say why.

Why did the man tell Mum there was no girl? Was it because he thought of 'girl' as 'child' and this girl is eighteen, which might mean 'woman' to him? She didn't look eighteen to me. And why didn't they mention her to the police?

If she isn't interested in making contact, if she's happy and busy – then why was she looking out of the window with such an unhappy expression? I can't help having the worst thoughts about why she's there. What if she's been kidnapped and is being held there against her will? What if she was abducted, like the woman I saw – and she's being held in that house and no one knows? No one, except me. The thought of it nags at me – it won't leave my head. I know it's unlikely – but what if it's true and I've known all this time but done nothing about it?

When I feel up to it, I browse online in short

spurts. I find a website called Missing People UK with a section on Missing Kids. I scroll down through the photos – so many children it scares me. Some are probably teenagers who've run away. Some look really young, though. What has happened to them? They must be somewhere. I glance for a few seconds at each face, as if I'll be able to find out their secrets. I look at the boys too as well as the girls. It feels wrong to miss anyone out – as if I'm saying that child is less important.

I find pictures of two Asian girls who *could* be the girl in the window. I try to think back to when I first saw her. Is it three months ago? One has only been missing for a month, so it can't be her. The other missing girl is called Farah Aziz. She is fifteen and has been missing for almost five months. She's from London too. She looks a bit angry in this picture, whereas the girl I see looks more sad, but the shape of her face, the dark hair – it really could be her. I search for her name and find a Facebook page dedicated to her, begging her to come home. There's a quote from her mother saying, 'We can work it out.'

My breath catches in my throat as I remember the reason I spotted the girl in the first place – the woman being dragged into the car. Perhaps something like that happened to Farah?

She might have been there all these months and I've been watching out of the window and she's been waiting – hoping I would rescue her and wondering why I keep looking out and looking out and yet doing nothing.

There is a number on the website. Dare I call it?

I decide I need to get a better look at her first – so I can be sure.

When the doorbell rings, she pushes me into the back room.
She takes the baby, rocking him in her arms, and she shuts
the door on me.

'Stay there,' she barks.

The baby cries instantly. He cries for me and I feel my
heart wrench for him. I want his warmth, his comfort, as
much as he wants mine.

I hear her voice as she opens the front door, sounding so
different from the voice she uses for me, or even for him. She
is polite and calm. I strain to hear what she's saying, what
is being said to her, but I cannot grasp the words. The baby's
noise is loud and my English is not so good. I wish I dared
open the door, just a crack, to hear better. But I dare not.

Then I hear the door shut and the baby's cries coming
nearer, and I stand back before she comes into the room, her
face blank and cold.

She hands the baby back to me and his crying stops
instantly. Only I can settle him when he cries. Only I can

tell his cries apart — the one for food and the one for hugs and the one for a clean nappy. She knows that. He is all that makes me human and not a ghost — the touch of his soft, soft skin, his small fingers tightly wrapped around mine, his eyes that follow me.

'We told you before — stay away from the windows,' she tells me. 'There are bad people out there. You want them to see you?'

Then she's gone.

13

I am still stuck upstairs and mainly in bed. I've not even been well enough to sit by the window, so I have no idea if the girl has appeared again. I don't have the focus to study. I haven't even started the homework Ellie brought, I can't do the small amount of work that Judy left for me and I can't even listen to audiobooks right now.

'I should have known those awards would be too much for you, *mój aniele*,' Mum worries. She puts a mug of tea down on my bedside cabinet and sighs.

'But it was amazing, Mum! I wanted to go and I'm glad I went. I just wish I didn't feel so bad now.'

'I know, you're right,' Mum says, nodding. 'Listen – I'm going to pop next door to check on Mrs Gayatri. I won't be long. Will you be OK?'

'Of course, Mum,' I say. 'Tell her I'll visit myself as soon as I can.'

'I'll tell her,' Mum assures me.

Mum really isn't gone for long, and she comes straight upstairs to see me when she's back.

'How's Mrs G?' I ask her.

'Not too bad,' Mum tells me. 'Her daughter's there – seems very nice. They were chatting away as if they'd never been apart. I've never seen Mrs G so animated. I met the grandson too, Navin – Nav, he likes to be called. He must be about your age.'

'What's he like?' I ask.

'I don't know. He didn't say much – sat playing on his phone, with earphones in. Mrs Gayatri says he's offered to sort out her garden this week, as it's half term, so that's good. She loves that garden but she hasn't been able to look after it properly for years. I did suggest to your dad once that he might mow it for her and he said he would when he had a chance, but of course he's never got round to it and he's so busy at work.'

Later I come out of the bathroom and hear the sound of the lawnmower out the back. I am curious and make my way to my parents' bedroom, clutching the walls as I go, so I can look out the back window. I sit on the dressing-table stool and peer down into Mrs G's garden.

I can see a boy with pale brown skin and dark brown hair sticking out from under a red beanie. He is mowing the overgrown lawn with Mrs Gayatri's mower, but is doing it in the most bizarre way I have ever seen. He's walking in zigzags, criss-crossing, sometimes going round in small circles. It's almost like a lawnmower waltz or something! I find myself laughing out loud, I can't help it. He's thorough, though, and it does look much neater when he's finished.

Next day I'm pleased to see he's there again. This time he's on a stepladder, trying to lop some dead wood out of an evergreen hedge with shears. The hedge is taking on a very weird shape and I start to wonder if he's actually doing topiary. I'm pleased I can remember the word for it — I remember Dad once describing hedges shaped like amazing birds in the garden of a big mansion he was extending. He showed me pictures online. Nav's hedge is starting to look like some kind of dinosaur, with a long curved back and spindly tail. Just as I think he's about to start work on the head, he chops it off, so maybe it wasn't meant to be a dinosaur after all.

'Nav seems like a nice boy,' says Mum, coming

in with a pile of washing. 'He's working so hard out there. Perhaps I'll suggest he comes round for a slice of cake and a drink. Wouldn't you like to meet him, Kasia?'

I wasn't expecting this. 'Mum! There's no way I can make it downstairs. Are you suggesting some strange boy comes up to my bedroom — with me in my pyjamas? I don't think so.'

Mum laughs at my expression. 'Kasia, don't be silly! You're bored and stuck indoors and I'm sure he could do with a break. You're curious about him, I can see, or you wouldn't have made the effort to walk all the way in here to look out the back window. I will help you get dressed.'

'In trackie bottoms and a hoodie?'

'Well, you're not going on a date, are you? That'll be fine for a chat and a snack.'

'You can suggest it to Mrs Gayatri if you want,' I say, sighing. 'He'll probably say no anyway.'

But he doesn't. Mum goes next door later that afternoon and comes back saying Nav will pop in tomorrow.

Now I'm feeling so nervous. Why did I agree? What are we going to talk about? I don't even know what time he's coming.

Next morning I get dressed slowly, the first time for ages, and then lie down for an hour. I look at myself in the mirror and try to cover up the spots that have flared up on my face. I brush my hair. It's so dry. It needs conditioner, but I don't have the energy to wash it very often and Mum has to help me.

He doesn't come. I wonder if he's changed his mind. I imagine him sitting with his earphones in, listening to music, playing some game on his phone. Surely he'd rather be doing that than coming round here to visit me. He must have just said yes to be polite.

Then the doorbell rings. I hear Mum greeting Nav cheerfully, but I don't hear his reply. I think about sitting in the chair, but decide to leave it for Nav. As I hear the footsteps on the stairs, I prop myself up with pillows.

'Come and meet Kasia,' Mum says brightly, pushing the bedroom door. She stands holding it open and Nav comes in. He's shorter than I thought – shorter than me – and he looks so nervous, as if I'm lying here dying or something. I'm only ill – I shouldn't be that terrifying.

'Can I get you a drink?' Mum asks him. 'A piece of apple cake?'

'I . . .'

'I'll bring you some,' Mum doesn't let him finish. 'Do you want anything, Kasia?'

'No thanks, Mum.'

'Sit down then and I'll leave you to get to know each other.'

Mum's gone. Nav sits awkwardly on the edge of the chair and I look at him. My room suddenly feels even smaller with this strange boy sitting here so close to me.

'Thanks for coming,' I say, though I'm not sure if I mean it yet.

'S'all right, not much else to do.' He shrugs but doesn't look up.

I wait for him to speak, but he clearly doesn't have a clue what to say.

'I saw you mowing the lawn,' I comment.

He looks startled. 'I thought you were stuck in here?'

'It varies from day to day,' I tell him. 'Some days I can get downstairs and others I am stuck in bed. I can get to the bathroom next door, and sometimes I make it to my parents' bedroom.'

'So you were spying on me?'

I'm not sure if he's teasing or if he's really embarrassed.

I nod and smile. 'Interesting way to mow a lawn! You never done one before?'

'No. We don't have a garden. I was just having a bit of fun. Looks all right, though, doesn't it?'

'Yeah, it looks fine. You did a good job.'

He meets my eyes properly for the first time.

'I'd love to have a garden,' he says. 'I got a Saturday job at the garden centre near where we live – just watering the plants and that – I thought it would be boring, but I really like it. I'm getting to know all the names and what soil different plants like. I want to study it – plants, garden design and all that.'

I have no interest in plants whatsoever, so I have never thought that someone might want to study them. I don't know anyone else my age that's interested in gardening.

'So maybe you take after your grandmother,' I say. 'She loves her garden.'

'I know. Hey, listen . . . I wanted to thank you – for finding Nani, you know? Saving her life. If it wasn't for you I'd never have got to meet her.'

Mum's head appears round the door.

'Here. Enjoy, Navin!' She hands over a plate with a large piece of apple cake and a fork.

'Thanks – that looks great,' he tells her.

'You taste – tell me what you think,' says Mum, and she's gone.

There's an awkward silence. Nav takes a bite of cake and brushes the crumbs from his mouth. I can see from his eyes he is more impressed than he expected to be with Mum's cake.

'So, you didn't even know your grandmother existed?' I blurt out.

Nav shrugs again and stares down at his plate. 'I knew she existed and I knew Mum never wanted to talk about her, that's all.'

'Sorry, I shouldn't have asked,' I say – though I'm hoping he will go on.

He doesn't.

'What's actually wrong with you then?' he suddenly asks. 'You don't look ill.'

I'm a bit stunned by the question. I thought I was being too personal, but now he is. Maybe he's deliberately getting his own back.

'I mean,' he goes on, 'Nani told me it was ME, but I don't really know what that is.'

'It stands for Myalgic Encephalomyelitis, and it started with a bad bout of tonsillitis,' I explain. 'I never properly got better. As soon as I do anything that requires any effort, I go backwards again. The pain in my legs, the pain I feel after walking, the dizziness, the swollen glands in my neck, the tiredness after doing the smallest thing – none of that shows. It's invisible. And I've been like this for eight months.'

'That's a long time,' he says.

I nod. 'I hate that I'm missing so much school, and that my friends are busy getting on with their lives and I'm not – it's like someone's pressed the pause button.'

'So what do you do all day?' he asks.

'Listen to the podcasts, audiobooks, look out of the window, try to study a bit when I can, think of ideas for stories I want to write.'

'You write stories?'

'Yes – I won a competition. That's the trophy.' I point at it on my desk, a bit worried that I am sounding boastful.

Nav strokes the trophy and looks genuinely

impressed. 'Nice,' he says. 'I'm not really a book person, me. I prefer films, you know? But you need to get out of here, girl. It can't be right being stuck indoors. Maybe you could sit outside and watch me gardening?'

I try not to laugh. I can't say that watching him weeding Mrs G's garden is much of an incentive, though I think he meant it kindly.

'I need time to recover from that award ceremony last week for the writing competition,' I tell him. 'What do you do when you're not gardening?'

'There's this game I play online — I play people all over the world.'

He starts to describe the game and I feel myself drifting off.

Nav suddenly stops. 'Hey – you look like you need a rest! Sorry – I was going on a bit. I hope I haven't made you feel worse?'

'No. It was nice of you to come,' I tell him. 'I hope you'll come again.'

14

Ellie comes over on her own the next day and I'm glad to have my best friend to myself again.

'What's new?' she asks.

'Not much,' I shrug. 'Mrs G next door – her daughter and grandson have come to stay. He's our age – he came round here yesterday.'

'What's he like?' Ellie asks eagerly.

'He's into gardening!' I tell her.

'Oh!' She makes a face. 'But he's tall and handsome?'

'Not tall – shorter than me. He was friendly enough though,' I add.

'Shame,' says Ellie. 'Bet you'd rather have Josh staying next door!'

I laugh.

'So the award ceremony knocked you out?' she says. 'It's such a shame. That trophy is so beautiful!'

'It was an amazing day,' I say, nodding, 'but I wish

I didn't have to suffer for it afterwards.'

'You were doing so well. I thought you'd be back at school soon,' Ellie comments. 'I wish they'd just find a pill you could take and that would be it – you'd be cured.'

'I wish that too,' I say with a sigh.

'Isn't there anything they can do?'

'Not much. I have to wait and see what the consultant says when I eventually see him.'

'Maybe you need a holiday – somewhere in the sun?' Ellie suggests. 'We're going to Spain in the summer, the same villa we went to last year. It's amazing, the pool is fab. Swimming might do you good too. Hey! Maybe you could come with us?'

'I'd love to, Ell – I'd love to so much – but I could never manage it. Think about how I've been since that short trip to the award ceremony. I could never cope with the journey to Spain – the airport, the plane, the journey the other end, or the heat. I'd be laid up in bed feeling vile and I'd have to shut all the blinds – the light would be so bright and I wouldn't feel well enough to even sit up.' Tears well up and I can't stop them sliding down my cheeks.

'Oh, Kasia. I'm so sorry! I didn't mean to make

you cry!'

'I can't believe I'll ever get better. Maybe I'll never be able to go on a plane again. Maybe I'll never get any qualifications. Maybe I'll never be able to work or marry Josh or have kids or anything.'

'Stop, stop!' Ellie holds out her arms to hug me. I let her, even though the hug hurts my muscles. 'You're *going* to get better, OK? Most people do, don't they?'

'Sorry, Ellie – just now and then it all builds up and I feel so frightened.'

'You'll be OK,' she tells me again. 'You've got me as a friend – your BFF, don't forget that! And I'm sure you'll get married one day, if that's what you really want, but it might not be to Josh. Do you know anyone who married someone they were at school with? I don't! Not many people do, I bet. Look, why don't we watch a film together – a funny one to cheer you up?'

'Thanks, Ellie. But I can't watch a screen for more than five minutes without getting a headache.'

I see Ellie's face drop and I force a smile.

'Anyway – enough!' I say. 'Let's talk about something else before I drown in self-pity! There's something I've been meaning to tell you.'

'Go on,' she says.

At last I tell her about the abduction, about the girl in the window, how the man and woman living there seem to be lying – even my mad ghost theory! Finally I show her the picture of Farah on the missing persons website.

Ellie's eyes are wide with astonishment as she peers at my tablet. 'So you really think this could be her – and that she's being kept across the road against her will?'

I nod. 'I think it's possible.'

'Are you going to call the police – or this missing persons helpline?' she asks.

'I don't feel sure enough,' I tell Ellie. The police didn't believe me about the abduction. I don't want to make a fool of myself.'

Ellie walks over to the window. 'She isn't there now,' she says.

'I haven't seen her since I went across the road and asked,' I admit. 'Maybe they're not letting her near the window. Or maybe she is eighteen and busy with the baby, like the woman said.'

'Next time you should take a picture on your phone,' says Ellie. 'Then you can zoom in and take a closer look. And perhaps there's another way to communicate with her. Could you put a note through the door?'

I shake my head. 'If the man or woman found it they'd never give it to her – and they would know I didn't believe them,' I say. 'But the photo's a good idea. I'll try that.'

'What else, what else . . .?' Ellie says thoughtfully. 'How about Morse code? You could flash with the torch on your phone.'

'I don't know Morse code,' I say doubtfully. 'And she might not either.'

'You can look it up online. It's worth a try.'

'I guess.' I nod again. 'Thanks Ellie – I'm glad I told you.'

After Ellie's gone, I look up Morse code and write out the signals for 'Do you need help?' I sit and watch at the window for as long as I can, but there's no sign of the girl.

15

The next day, Nav comes round with a book. It's called *Recovering from Chronic Fatigue*. I thank him and put it on my desk. Mum got a few books out of the library when I was diagnosed, but they weren't much help. This one looks better but it's a heavy book and I know it will give me pains in my arms if I hold it for too long. Whoever wrote or published it didn't think about that! It's nice of him, though.

'My mum spotted it in that discount bookshop on the High Street,' he tells me. 'And I've been reading it myself. Just call me Dr Navin – here to get you well!'

I laugh a bit but I'm also surprised. He's been reading it – to help me. That's thoughtful and kind.

'I won't need to read it then,' I joke. 'It's a bit heavy anyway.'

'No, it's quite easy to read,' he tells me.

'I mean the weight of it, not the content!'

He laughs. 'Rest it on your pillow!'

'So what's the advice, doc?'

'It's all about routine,' Nav says. 'You do the same every day – only half of what you feel up to doing, what you can do without feeling worse. Then you very, very gradually increase that over time. It's all about recharging your batteries, you see? Like your illness has made them flat, and they need to be charged. Light activity will begin to recharge them.'

'Sounds like the pacing I already do,' I say.

'But it's not regular, is it? I think you do much more some days and then you're laid up afterwards. Isn't that right?'

'Yes. When there are things I really want to do – you know, like the writing award ceremony. I know I'll suffer afterwards, but it's worth it.'

'I think you should try the suggestions in this book – along with my help, of course. If you do it gradually, it should stop you having so many setbacks. And I prescribe that spending time outside in the fine weather, watching me gardening next door, will be the best treatment ever!'

'It's not exactly fine, the weather,' I say, looking out at the cloudy sky.

'But it will get better!' he assures me. 'It's quite

warm today — no chill in the air. Come on.'

'What, *now*?'

'No time like the present, as my mother always says when she wants me to tidy my room!'

'I am feeling a bit better today. I was thinking about going downstairs. But . . .'

'No buts. You have a fleece or something?'

I'm wearing trackie bottoms and a T-shirt. 'I thought you said it was warm.'

'Warm if you dress right. Come on. Take my arm if you like.'

'No, it's OK. I can manage.'

I find myself on my feet, grabbing my zip-up from the wardrobe and pulling it on. I follow Nav down the stairs and for once manage to not pause for breath halfway. I worry instantly — is that a good thing or have I overdone it already?

Nav opens the front door.

'I need to tell Mum I'm going out,' I protest.

'It's done — she knows,' he says, and before I can object to the fact that they've been conspiring together, I am outside.

I follow Nav round to the garden gate next door and into the garden. There's still a chill wind, but I like the feel of the sun on my back when it peeps out from behind the clouds. As I stand on the patio my legs begin to ache and I look round anxiously for a bench or a small wall to perch on. There's nothing.

'Nav – I don't think . . . I need to sit down. I'd better go back.'

'No need – I'll have a chair out of the shed in two secs. Should have done that first!' He jogs down the garden and returns with a garden chair, which he quickly unfolds for me.

Now that I'm sitting and not panicking I can look at the garden properly. The lawn is now fine but although Nav's done some pruning, there are still lots of overgrown and unwieldy shrubs. Long wispy branches swing wildly in the gentle breeze as if they are looking for something to hold on to. A few daffodils have opened and some flowering bushes are stretching up to find light, like children trying to see over a wall.

'It looks like it needs a lot of work,' I say.

'You're right,' Nav agrees, but he says it cheerfully and not downheartedly, as I might do if confronted by a challenge like this.

'I wish I was here for longer so I could really get

stuck in,' he says. 'Nani's shown me photos from years ago, when my grandfather was still alive. They both loved this garden and it was beautiful. Would you like to see?'

'Sure,' I nod.

Nav is quiet for a moment.

'You look sad,' I tell him.

'Just thinking about how weird but great it is getting know my grandmother, and wishing I could have met my grandfather. Do you have grandparents?'

I shake my head. 'I did — in Poland. *Babcia*, my gran, was the only one I met, and she died last year. I was sad but I didn't know her well — visiting once or twice a year wasn't enough to get really close. Mum was really upset, though.'

I pause, then blurt out a question that I'm sure Mum would say was too personal. 'If you don't mind me asking, what about your dad?'

Nav shrugs. 'Never knew him — my grandparents didn't approve as he wasn't a Hindu so Mum took off with him and cut contact with them. She was a bit of rebel, my mum. Then when she found out she was pregnant, my dad went off and left her. I've never felt bothered about trying to find him cos he clearly had no interest in me. Mum didn't feel like crawling back to her parents so she stayed away. Now she's back with Nani, she regrets the way they fell out and all the time they lost, especially as they're getting on so well!'

'Something good came out of your gran's stroke then?'

'Yes – and that's thanks to you, isn't it?' He smiles.

He looks down towards the back of the garden. 'Now, shall I take you on a tour?' he asks me.

'Tour?' I look down the garden which stretches to at least 30 metres. 'I'm not . . . I can't . . .'

'Negativity!' he interrupts. 'The enemy of progress and recovery.'

'It's not negativity, it's realism,' I argue. 'If I overdo it, I relapse. That's a fact that I've learnt from experience.'

'Who's talking about overdoing it?'

'A tour – that's what you said.'

'A tour of the patio!' He grins.

'Oh. You should have said.'

'You must worry less, Kasia. Anxiety is also your enemy. Now, can I get you a drink? Are you warm enough? I can fetch one of Nani's blankets for your knees?'

He's seen me shudder slightly at the breeze. 'Please stop fussing, Nav. I'm OK.' I can't bear the thought of sitting with a blanket over my knees like an old lady. I'm beginning to wish I'd stayed at home but once Nav starts some frenetic pruning I can't help laughing and he clearly enjoys having an audience.

When he's finished, we walk round the patio. I have to sit down again after a couple of minutes, but he carries on talking, telling me his plans for the garden. I have no idea what plants he's talking about but I love his enthusiasm for it all.

Mrs G comes out later, bringing her photos to show me. Nav fetches another chair for her.

'My garden is helping to tear my grandson away from his small screen games,' she says with a smile.

'Nah, I can do both,' Nav teases her. 'Garden all day, game all night.'

I look at the photos and am amazed to see an exotic-looking, flower-filled garden. 'It's incredible! It doesn't look like the same garden!'

'We tried to recreate the gardens of our childhoods in India,' she tells me. 'Of course, many of the plants there won't grow here, but we went for the bright colours we loved.'

'I'd love to restore it,' says Nav. 'The school holidays don't give enough time to do a proper job, but least I can make a start.'

'Where's your daughter?' I ask Mrs G. 'Doesn't she want to sit out too?'

'Devi's next door,' she tells me, 'chatting with your mother.'

When I come home I find them sitting in our kitchen eating cake. I immediately like the look of Devi and I can see she has the same smile as Mrs G.

'Hi, you must be Kasia,' Devi says cheerfully. 'My mum told me about your mother's cakes and she's right. Your mum's a talented baker. She should be entering the *Bake-Off* on TV!'

'Sit with us, Kasia – try some,' says Mum, smiling.

I really want to go and lie down, but I decide to stay for a minute. 'Just a small piece, Mum,' I say. 'Is it one of Gran's mystery recipes?'

'Yes – it's poppy seed cake. It's not as good as Gran's, though.'

I sit and she places a small piece on a plate in front of me. I take a bite.

'It's delicious, Mum.'

I look from Mum to Devi. Mum is looking happier and more animated than I've seen her for ages. It occurs to me how isolated she must have been feeling, cut off from her friends at work and stuck at home, caring for me. I like Devi and Mum clearly does too. She has a vibrancy, an energy about her, even though she's sitting still. She's wearing a top covered in colourful flowers – red, purple and orange, like the photo of Mrs G's garden. I think she will be a good friend for Mum.

That evening, as I'm closing the curtains, I look out – and I see her. The girl. The room behind her is dark, but she's there and she doesn't vanish.

I grab my phone and unfold the paper on the windowsill where I've written the Morse code. Using the torch I flash the signal for 'Do you need help?', and I have to concentrate hard to make sure I do it right.

By the time I've finished, she's gone. I wonder if she understood any of it. Maybe she's gone to get a torch – or her phone or iPad to look up what it means. She'll surely come back.

I wait and wait but she doesn't come. Perhaps flickering lights give her a headache, like they do with some people with ME. Or maybe she can't cope with the light at all. A vampire? I can't help laughing at myself for having this thought. I just wish I knew what was going on.

She shone a light. What was she was doing? Flashing and flashing. She must not do this. She mustn't. Was she trying to say something?

Later I think maybe it is a code. A code with lights — I think I have heard of such a thing. But I have no torch to reply, no way to look up any code. Maybe it isn't a code.

Yet I am happy that she knows I am here. She cares. Perhaps she only wants to tell me that there is light — that this darkness will one day end. I hope she is right.

16

I am out in Mrs G's garden with Nav. It's a Saturday in March and the garden is scattered with daffodils. Nav is planting bulbs that he says will come up in the summer. He seems to have stacks of them. I look at the labels and pictures.

'Will they really look like this?' I ask. 'It'll be amazing.'

'I hope so!' says Nav, grinning. 'Come and see the magnolia. It's half hidden but the flowers are lovely already.'

He has pruned back some of the bushes a bit roughly, but enough so that when I stop and look through the gap I can see a tree in a clearing, clustered with pink flowers.

I reach for a low hanging bloom and breathe in. 'It's like perfume,' I tell him. Then the scent catches my throat and I have to step away. I can't even tolerate nice smells these days.

'I want to grow lots of herbs and veg too,' Nav tells me. 'And I'll plant more stuff at the end of May – when there's no risk of frost. Nani's been sharing her knowledge – and a couple of good gardening books too! I've got a lot to learn, though.'

'You'll be back in May then?' I ask.

'Yes, and most weekends too, maybe more. My mum's getting all emotional about Nani, saying we should come and look after her,' Nav tells me. 'They are getting on so well I don't think they want to be apart. They want to make up for lost time.'

'What – move in?'

He nods.

'Do you want to?' I ask.

He shrugs. 'I've got friends and that, where we're living, but it's a poky flat. Nani's garden – that makes it tempting . . . Oh and having you next door, of course!'

I make a face.

'What? You don't want your "doctor" living next door?' he teases.

I try to imagine what it would be like having Nav living next door. I've never had a neighbour my age.

'Oh – I'd probably have to go to your school too,'

he says. 'What's it like?'

'Can hardly remember — haven't been there for ages!' I comment. 'But if you do end up there, I can tell you who to avoid and that kind of stuff.'

He smiles. 'Thanks.'

'If you stay, which bedroom will be yours — is it at the front, like mine?'

'Yes — that's where I'm sleeping now,' he tells me.

'Have you ever seen anyone across the road, looking out the window?' I ask.

He shakes his head. 'I don't look out much,' he says. 'Why?'

'Can I tell you something,' I ask, 'something a bit weird?'

'Go on,' he says, looking intrigued.

I tell him about the girl and why I'm worried about her. I tell him how the couple denied she existed and then said she was their eighteen-year-old niece. I tell him about the abduction I saw and how I think the girl saw too. I don't tell him I thought she was a ghost.

'It does sound odd,' he says. 'I haven't seen her but I'll have to keep a look out.'

'I keep worrying about her,' I explain, 'and then telling myself she must be OK because all the things I'm imagining – that she's been kidnapped or something like that – seem too far-fetched. But I really want to know the truth.'

'Maybe you could wait until the couple go out and then try again,' Nav suggests. 'You could go and knock – see if she'll come to the door and speak to you. Then you'll get a proper look at her and find out if she's OK. And you can ask her about that woman and the car – whether she saw anything.'

'I could,' I say. 'It can't do any harm to try.'

'I'll come with you, if you like?' says Nav.

'Really? Thanks.'

'I'll give you my number and you can text me when you know the people are out. If I'm free, I'll come.'

For the rest of the day and on Sunday I keep an even closer watch on the house, until I finally see the couple come out, get into the white car and drive off.

I text Nav.

'Meet out the front in five,' he texts back.

It takes me more than five minutes but Nav is waiting for me when I finally get there. We cross the road and I ring the bell on the shabby red front door.

'Keep an eye out,' I tell him. 'Just in case they

come back.'

There's no answer. I ring again. Then I look through the letterbox. Unlike Mrs G's there is no letter guard – just a hole. It is easier to see in, but there's nothing to see except two closed doors and the staircase.

'Is anyone there?' I call. 'It's Kasia from across the road. I just want to know if you're OK.'

We wait. 'If she's there, I don't think she's coming,' says Nav.

Then I hear a baby's cry. Nav's eyes shift to the right. He heard it too.

'They didn't take the baby!' I explain. I saw them go – and I didn't think about it. They left the baby here. So the girl must be in there. They can't have left the baby alone, can they?'

'Call again,' says Nav.

I do.

Still there is no answer apart from the distant baby cries.

'We'll have to leave it,' Nav says, shaking his head. 'Sometimes people just don't like answering the door.'

I don't want to – but I know he's right and my legs feel like they're going to give, anyway.

'We'll try again another time,' Nav says.

She rang the bell. I did not know who it was. The door is locked — 'to keep me safe'. Bad people might come. Then I heard her voice. I heard her say, 'It is Kasia — from across the road.' So now I know her name, a pretty name, Kasia. She is my friend — my only friend, come to call for me.

How good it would be to open the door, to invite her in, to make tea and have cake and sit and chat with her, show her the baby, and she'd coo at him and squeeze his chubby legs.

She had someone with her. I heard her talking to someone. Trust no one. That's what they tell me. It was a male voice. Who was he? Maybe he is the bad person they spoke of. Maybe he's come to take me to another place — a far worse place than this.

It does not matter because the door is locked. I have no key. Does she not realise — the girl, Kasia — that I have no key?

17

I don't want it to go to Nav's head but I think the advice from the book he gave me is making a difference. I am managing to come downstairs every day and even to do some of the work Judy has given me.

Nav has gone back home but we text each other every day. I miss him being next door and am pleased when he says he'll be back on Friday for the weekend.

He texts me as soon as he arrives and I'm happy to be back out in the garden with him.

'Guess what? You are going to be seeing a lot more of me! We are moving here to live with Nani.'

'Wow! That's great. Mrs G must be so happy!'

'And I hope you are too!' he teases. 'Mum was worried about me changing schools now I've started my GCSE classes, but your school has assured her it will all be fine.'

'So you'll be in my year?'

'Yes. I'll start after Easter. It would be better,

of course, if you were there to show me round.'

'I wish I could.'

We're both quiet for a moment. I won't be able to show him round at school but I think I'm going to like having him next door.

'You can tell me things I need to know and I'll tell you what's going on,' he says. 'And you will be back there soon. That is Dr Nav's ambition!'

'Mine too!' I tell him.

'For now, though, I need your help with this garden.'

I look at him doubtfully.

'Wait here.'

He hurries to the house and comes back with what looks like a magazine.

'Plant catalogue,' he says, handing it to me. 'I want to plant new flowering shrubs and rescue as many as I can from what's here. I've already planted bulbs, and I plan to sow seeds on a big scale so there will be an amazing display of flowers for the summer. Gran says I can get a mini-greenhouse – a plastic one – so I can grow some seeds there now and plant out the seedlings in May. I will get some plant plugs too – small plants, ready to go straight in the ground.'

'What do you want me to do?' I ask. I flick through and beautiful flowers leap from the pages. I have no idea what most of them are.

'You can help me choose. Anything colourful or exotic-looking. You know the kind of thing Nani likes. While I edge the border, you take this pen and circle anything you like.'

I feel a lovely sense of calm as I browse through the catalogue, glancing up frequently to watch Nav chopping the border with an edging tool. He does not seem to like straight lines and is curving it in a very attractive way. A robin is sitting on the fence watching too and a few other birds are twittering cheerfully by the bird feeder. It really is starting to feel like spring now and I feel a renewed optimism.

'I need a drink,' he tells me. He goes in and brings out two glasses of juice, then sits down beside me.

'Seen anything you like?' he asks.

'I like these Rudbeckias – and the dahlias,' I tell him.

'Good choices – I love them too.' He grins. 'I want to get a bench as well, with a bower over it, so Nani can relax where there is warm sun, but also a little shade. I'm watching out on auction sites and

Mum has said she'll pay if I can find one that's not too expensive.'

'I like the way you've done the edge of the border — all curvy,' I comment. 'It looks much nicer than when it was just straight.'

'I saw it in this garden book. It shows you how to add mirrors to make it look even bigger. That's something I'm thinking about.'

'I can't wait to see it in the summer,' I say.

'I can picture it so clearly in my mind,' Nav replies. 'I hope I can make it happen.'

'I'm sure you can,' I say.

I last for a whole two hours in the garden, before I have to go home and lie down for a while. I even do some studying in the evening. I'm so pleased Nav is moving in next door but a little bit of me is worried that they may have given him my place at school because they think I won't be coming back. Inside, I hope that's just me thinking the worst again.

On Monday Ellie and Lia come by on their way back from rehearsals, full of the show — which is just before the Easter break, less than two weeks away — and how brilliant it is going to be.

'You will come, won't you?' Ellie demands. 'You're so much better now.'

I discuss it with Mum and Dad. They agree in the end that I can go to the show but come straight back afterwards. Dad will drive me and I'm to call him to pick me up the moment it ends.

I mention to Nav that I'm going and to my surprise he asks if he can come too. I'm not sure how I feel about that – I'm happy for him to come, but I know that one of the reasons I want to go is to see Josh. I hope that won't be too obvious.

On the day, I make an effort with jeans and a nice top I haven't worn for nearly a year. I manage to wash my hair and Mum blow-dries it for me.

'There, you look almost human!' she teases.

I look in the mirror and am pleased with what I see. Even my skin is getting healthier-looking.

Dad and Nav both compliment me on how I look. Dad drives me and Nav to school and is full of reminders about calling when it finishes so he can pick me up. We pass the staircase where I panicked last time I was here, all those months ago, and I glance up at it. I'm sure I could manage those stairs now but I'm still glad the show is on the ground floor.

I sit with Nav in the second row. Some people give me strange looks – perhaps they're surprised to see me or they wonder who this boy is that I'm with. Bethany and Amy from my form group come up smiling, saying it's nice to see me. I'm surprised, because they've never been that friendly.

Then they sit two rows behind and I can hear them whispering loudly about me. 'Thought she was ill? She looks fine.' I don't turn to look but I know that's Amy's voice. 'How come she's well enough for a show and not well enough for school?'

'Too right!' That's Bethany. 'Anyway, my dad says there's no such things as ME. It's all in your head.'

Nav gives me a look. He's heard them too and looks as if he's going to say something back.

I shake my head. 'They're not my friends,' I tell him. 'Just ignore them.'

'I hope they're not all like that here,' says Nav.

Before I can reply Miss Giles comes over, saying she's pleased to see me not needing a wheelchair and hopes I'll be back at school soon. She talks enthusiastically about the award again and I start to feel better.

Then Erin and Tilly, who I thought *were* my friends,

but who I haven't seen for months, shuffle over to say hi.

'Good to see you!' Erin tells me. 'I'm sorry I haven't been in touch. I'm a bit useless around sick people.'

I'm not sure what to say to this, so instead I introduce them to Nav and they start talking to him.

The seats are hard and although it's embarrassing I'm glad Mum made me bring a cushion. I wouldn't have lasted three minutes otherwise.

A few more people come over to say hi and tell me how well I'm looking.

'Seem like a friendly bunch,' Nav says, 'apart from those two losers behind.'

I nod. I almost feel like a fraud, I feel so normal. Maybe I will be back at school sooner than I thought.

The lights go down and the concert begins. To my delight, I am close to where Josh is sitting in the orchestra and I have a perfect view of him. I keep hoping he'll glance up and see me. If he'd only look at me – meet my eyes, give me a friendly wink or nod or smile – it would completely make my day. But he doesn't. He's quite rightly focused on the music and concentrating with every breath.

Ellie and Lia have small roles in the show, but perform them impressively and are clearly enjoying themselves.

'Wow! That was so good!' I tell Ellie, when she comes out. I introduce Nav and she says hi.

She looks at her watch. 'It isn't even late, there's a party now – the after-show party. Will you come – just for a little while? Nav, you'll stay too, won't you?'

Nav hesitates. 'It's up to you, Kasia. I'll stay if you want to.'

I glance round to see Josh putting his violin in its case. I don't have the energy or nerve to go over now, though I'd love to tell him how good the show was, how good *he* was. I imagine him smiling, his whole face lighting up as I speak.

Feeling a bit guilty, I turn back to Nav. 'Just for a few minutes,' I agree. 'I don't want to overdo it.'

'Great, come on then,' says Nav. 'You can introduce me to some more people.'

Nav and I follow Ellie, leaving Josh still packing up his violin and chatting to some sixth-formers.

We reach the canteen where the party is being held. The room's been cleared and there aren't many chairs out. My worst fear is that there will be nowhere to sit down. I am still clutching my cushion and get a few odd glances. I want to put the cushion on a chair and sit on it as quickly as possible.

'Nav . . .' I begin, but I don't even need to finish as he's there with a chair he's grabbed from somewhere. I just hope he didn't tip anyone off it in his haste.

'Thanks,' I say.

He grins. 'I'll get us some drinks. He turns to Ellie. 'What would you like?'

He goes off to get Ellie a coke and me some water, and Ellie watches him, chuckling.

'What?' I demand.

'It's like he thinks he's your carer or something – fussing over you like that. Don't you find him annoying?'

I feel instantly irritated with Ellie. 'No, I don't,' I say firmly.

More people are coming in and the room is getting crowded. I'm starting to feel hot and a bit dizzy. I'm relieved when Nav comes back with the drinks.

We chat with Ellie, Tia and Erin and I introduce Nav to a few boys from our year. Then the others go off to mingle and I'm left with Nav.

'I hope I can get back to playing the cello,' I tell

him. 'I should have been in this show. I loved being in the orchestra.'

'I'd really like to hear you play,' says Nav.

'I want to get back to playing, but I can't even lift it now,' I say.

'One day you will,' he assures me. 'Maybe you'll even play in next year's concert.'

'I'm getting stronger all the time,' I say, nodding. He gives me a sweet smile and I smile back.

Then I see Josh has come in. There is a kind of aura around him, an energy that's almost like a beam of light. For a moment he's on his own, looking around. I wonder if he'll see me. I want to get up and go over to him, but I don't dare – what if he doesn't remember me at all?

Then a girl goes up to him. They're talking. I don't know her name, but she's in the same year as Josh. He's smiling and nodding. Is he with her? Are they together?

'So?'

Nav has asked me something and I've missed it completely.

'What? Sorry?'

'I think maybe we should go now? Are you going

144

to text your dad?'

I look at my watch and notice with horror that it's after eleven. How did that happen? I pull out my phone and see three unread messages and three missed calls from my dad. He's not going to be happy.

And I am right. He is furious when he arrives — with Nav as well as me.

'I'm so sorry,' Nav tells him as we get in the car. 'But I think Kasia's fine. I've been looking after her. She's been sitting down the whole time.'

'I think I'm OK, Dad,' I tell him. 'I had fun — I almost felt normal for the first time in months. Please don't be angry.'

'We said clearly that you could go, but to text me straight after,' Dad reminds me. 'There was no mention of a party! We would never have agreed to that. Why do you ignore us? We say it for good reason — for your health!'

Dad sounds so disappointed I feel wretched. I hate letting him down.

'I didn't mean to ignore your messages. I just . . . I mean, I lost track of time. I'm sure I'll be OK, though — I feel fine.'

'We'll see,' says Dad. 'I hope you're right.'

Nav gives me a big smile and squeezes my hand as we part. 'I'll see you tomorrow.'

I walk quickly upstairs to bed, keen to show Dad that I am fine. My legs are actually not too bad, and I am buzzing with excitement. Normal life, school, friends – everything that's felt so far away suddenly feels much closer.

18

The next day I wake up and I check my body for pain. Legs – some pain, but not too bad, arms – the same. Head quite clear. I sit up gingerly and then stand. I am OK. Not brilliant, but no major relapse. I am delighted.

Nav texts to check I'm OK and I'm relieved to tell him I feel fine.

'See – your dad was wrong! Going to the show was good for you,' he tells me. 'As well as giving me the chance to meet lots of people before I start at your school.'

'I wish I was ready to start back too,' I reply. 'But at least it feels like it will be possible one day.'

The following day I wake up and find I can't move at all. I am too weak to sit up and my legs are throbbing. I feel completely wiped out. It's a delayed reaction and I should have known it would happen. Why do I never learn? And I hate that Dad was right.

I can't walk. I can't get out of bed. And it's not just for one day. I'm worse than I was when I was bed-bound before and I feel so depressed. It isn't fair. It just isn't fair.

I feel so bad I start to blame Nav for encouraging me. Even the fact that I saw Josh doesn't cheer me up any more. Seeing him with that girl didn't help — they're probably going out together now. I feel helpless and so, so alone.

One night, Mum comes to check on me on her way to bed and I pretend to be asleep as I don't have the energy to speak or even open my eyes.

'Yes, she's asleep,' she tells Dad. I hear their bedroom door close, but within minutes I can hear them arguing — and it's about me.

'We should never have let her go,' says Dad. 'Look what she's done to herself — and after all that progress!'

'It's understandable that she wants to do these things — to be with her friends,' says Mum.

'But she knows full well what happens when she does too much. She has to take responsibility. And so do you. Why aren't you phoning the doctors, the hospital, to insist on some proper treatment? You accept what the doctors tell you – you let her lie forgotten on a waiting list!'

'That's not fair,' Mum protests. 'I'm the one caring for her all day, every day. I gave up my job to do that. I want her well and back to school just as much as you do. I have phoned several times and they say there's nothing they can do – others have been waiting longer. I even looked into going private, but we can't afford it.'

'Why is this happening to us?' Dad groans. 'What have we done to deserve it? We move country, we both work hard – all hours to make a good life for our children. And all we have is one drop-out, good-for-nothing son and a daughter who can't get out of bed.'

'Oh, Stefan – you can't think like that,' Mum tells him. 'These things happen.'

'But why to US?' Dad yells. I hear a thud. I think he's thrown a book or something. It's rare for Dad to get so angry. He's my comedian – the one who makes me laugh. I hate that he feels like this. I don't cry often but I can't help it now. I lie there, crying into my pillow.

I stay in bed for two more weeks. Nav texts and so

does Ellie but I don't feel like replying.

Nav is persistent, but I don't answer. I feel too low. Then I get this message from him:

'Coming over – don't move!'

Before I can tell Mum I don't want any visitors, I hear the bell ring, followed by heavy footsteps running up the stairs.

'Hi,' he says, sitting down in the window chair. I am in bed, slightly propped up.

'Hi,' I say back.

There's an awkward silence. 'So, I think I saw that girl,' he tells me, 'looking out of the window across the road.'

'Really?' I ask. I immediately feel guilty as I've kind of stopped thinking about her. I've not been well enough to look out.

'Anyway, I've just seen the couple go out,' he says. 'So I thought you might like to try again. You know, go and knock on the door.'

'I'm not up to it, am I?' I huff.

'I can see that,' he says. 'Well, when you are, we can try again. Dr Nav thinks you should start building up your stamina again, taking it gradually.'

I am not in the mood for his cajoling. 'Dr Nav

should stop sticking his nose in to my business.'

He looks at me, his face dropping. 'I'm sorry this happened,' he says. 'I can't believe you've ended up like this after just one night out.'

'I should never have gone,' I say angrily. 'I certainly shouldn't have stayed afterwards.'

'It was a mistake,' he says, nodding.

'But you encouraged me!'

His eyes are wide. 'Because it was what you wanted. It was your decision. It's not fair for you to blame me.'

'Well I do!'

I'm not sure why I'm saying that. I don't really blame him – but he's making me angry. He thinks he knows it all – he made me feel that if I stayed for the party I'd be OK. And now he's walking in here, uninvited, talking as if it's no big deal.

'Why?' Nav looks really hurt now, but I can't seem to get past my anger.

'You made me believe! All this "come downstairs, come out in the garden, see how much progress you're making, you'll soon be back at school . . ." You gave me hope, Nav. And it was a waste of time.'

'Sorry I bothered,' he mutters. 'I thought you liked

being with me. I thought we were friends.'

'I've got friends, Nav. I don't need you.'

He stares at me, clearly shocked. I have shocked myself too. I should take it back, I should say sorry. But Nav turns and walks out. I hear his feet thud on the stairs and then the front door closing.

'Everything OK?' Mum says, putting her head round my door.

'I didn't feel like seeing anyone. You shouldn't have let him up here,' I tell her, switching off the bedside lamp.

'What happened?' Mum sits on the edge of the bed in the dark, but my head is spinning and I just want to close my eyes and pretend all this isn't happening.

'I need to sleep, Mum. I don't want to talk about it.'

'Later then,' she says, but I have no intention of talking about it at all.

True to my stubborn word, I still won't talk about Nav the next day, no matter how much Mum presses me.

'I talked to Devi. She says Nav is very upset. What's going on?'

'Leave it, Mum,' I tell her.

Eventually she sits back and sighs. 'Kasia,' she says, 'you seem very low and you're so isolated. I know you have Ellie, but she's busy now studying. I think you need some support. How about looking online for a support group?'

'I looked once and it was full of middle-aged people who've been ill for longer than I've been alive,' I remind her.

'But I contacted an ME charity and they told me there's a Facebook group for teenagers.'

'I'm not going to be cheered up by talking to other people who are as miserable as I am, Mum,' I protest. 'What's the point?'

'You may feel less alone,' says Mum. 'I'm worried about you.'

'I don't want you to worry,' I tell her.

'Then you'll have a look, just to keep me happy?' she pleads.

So I look. Although I know there are lots of teenagers with ME, I haven't actually met any. And I'm surprised to find Mum is right. I sign up to the group, but have to wait for 'approval' before I can see the posts.

The following day I am notified I can access the closed group. I start reading the posts.

There's Dina, who is my age and has been ill for four years. She can cope with half days at school and is still managing to work for five GCSEs, but is finding it very hard. 'People still think I'm faking it, after all this time!' she writes. 'They don't understand why I get to go home early. They wouldn't be jealous if they knew how ill I felt and how frustrating it is not to be able to stay at school all day.'

Then there's Ariana who's been bedbound for two years, but is able to look at a screen for short bursts. She uses a phone – she doesn't have the strength to hold a tablet – and only uses it for the support group. She is desperate for help, and her mum keeps phoning hospitals and doctors and organisations, but there's nothing on offer.

Some people have been offered Cognitive Behavioural Therapy (CBT) and pacing and physio, and something called the Lightning Process. Others have tried alternative therapies, like acupuncture and healing. With all these things, there are some people saying they helped – but also some who feel worse after trying them.

A girl called Mimi has posted a poem she's written about having ME. It's sad but also funny and makes me laugh. I 'like' it and comment that I enjoy writing too, but mostly stories and I'm not well enough to write anything at the moment.

Later I see she's replied, asking me if I'm new to the group and encouraging me to try poetry as it's shorter. She asks me if I like reading too and recommends a book.

Although it's depressing to read about people like Ariana, I am happy to have found people who understand exactly what it's like – especially Mimi.

A few days later I am a little better. On my way back from the bathroom I go to the window and briefly glance out. I see Nav walking back from the shops with a bag of shopping. The good grandson, shopping for his Nani. Bitterness fills my mouth, sour as lemons. I am so full of anger still and somehow it is all directed at Nav. He doesn't even glance up as he goes back inside.

I lie half listening to a local music station online. The news comes on – and I'm not really paying attention until the words 'attempted abduction' catch my ear. Then I start listening properly because the case they're speaking about happened quite near here.

A man started talking to a sixteen-year-old girl who was walking home from school. He asked her the time and then started chatting, asking if she knew where he could buy cigarettes. As they turned the corner the man got out a key and opened a parked car and tried to push the girl into it. She struggled and luckily managed to poke him in the eye and run off.

I think back to the night when I saw what looked like a woman being abducted. Could there be a connection? The car described was a different colour and this one happened in broad daylight, but is it too much of a coincidence? I wish the police had reported back on whether they'd found out anything.

I get up and look out of the window. The girl across the road isn't there. I've not been looking as much but I haven't seen her for ages. Nav said he saw her, so she's still in the house. I wonder again if she is being kept prisoner. But she can't really be Farah, can she – that girl from the missing persons website?

19

It's a few more days before I feel well enough to get out of bed and move around regularly. One day I hear the sound of the lawnmower and I walk to the back bedroom and look out. The garden next door is looking so much better now. Nav has dug up a lot of the old half-dead shrubs and planted new ones, and more are beginning to flower. He definitely has an eye for colour. He is mowing in straight lines today and I feel strangely disappointed. Is it because I upset him? I feel a plum-sized bulge of guilt in my throat. He didn't deserve the way I spoke to him. I text him:

'So sorry about what I said.'

I look out and see him pull his phone from his trouser pocket. I wait expectantly for him to text back or even to look up in the window, but he puts the phone back in his pocket and carries on mowing.

I realise I should apologise in person, but I'm not in the mood today. Also, deep down, I think I'm scared he may not accept my apology. He'd have every right not to – after what I said. I miss him.

On the first day of summer term, I hear Mrs G's front door open and close, and Devi's voice calling, 'Good Luck!' I get out of bed and pull the curtain aside to see Nav in school uniform walking down the road. His walk is bouncy, as if he's really looking forward to it. I wish so much that I was going too. Right now I can't imagine that will ever happen.

That afternoon the doorbell rings and a part of me almost hopes it's Nav – but it's Ellie who runs up the stairs and into my room. It's lovely to see her, and though I'm still really down I feel my spirits lift slightly.

'Hi, chick,' she says, bouncing down on to my bed and sending me jerking up as if I'm on a trampoline. 'I've got news for you.'

'What news?' I ask half-heartedly.

She leans forward and smiles. 'You're not going to believe this, Kasia!'

'Spit it out then.'

'Josh – he came up to me today. He asked me about you!'

'What?' I sit up. Now this really *is* news. 'When? How come? What did he say?'

'He asked how you are, whether I still see you, when you're coming back to school. He was pleased when I said you were getting better. I didn't tell him you got worse after the concert.'

'It's weird that he's asking now, after all this time!' I say. 'I thought he'd forgotten I exist. Maybe he saw me there.'

'You still like him, right?' Ellie asks. 'Do you want me to tell him you're interested?'

I reel back in horror. 'Don't you dare!'

'OK – keep your hair on. I was only offering!'

But my mind is whirring with cinematic images of us together – of his arms reaching out towards me, his beaming smile.

'You're still into him, aren't you?' Ellie smiles. 'I can see it in your eyes.'

I feel myself blush. 'I like him, Ellie. OK? But I saw him with a girl at the concert. I thought they were together.'

'Who? Was it Chloe? Nah, they're just friends,' says Ellie.

New motivation tingles inside me like fizzy

lemonade. 'I'm going to pace myself. I'll set myself targets and build up gradually, and be extra careful about not overdoing it. I'm going to get better and I'm going to tell him exactly how I feel – I won't be shy this time. And I'm going to get back to school, too.'

Ellie smiles again. 'Good for you.'

We chat for a bit longer, and then Ellie gets up to go. She turns to me before she leaves. 'Oh, Kasia, have you seen anything of that weird girl at the window you told me about? I keep forgetting to ask you.'

'I've not been well enough to look out much, so no,' I tell her. 'But what I said about her being that girl on the website – it's crazy, isn't it? The woman was probably telling the truth – the girl's eighteen, but looks young for her age and is there helping with the baby.'

'Really?' Ellie asks. 'You were so suspicious before.'

I shrug. 'To be honest, I don't know what to think.'

After Ellie's gone, I sit by the window, trying to work out how long it is since I saw the girl. Then suddenly – as if she's reading my thoughts – she's there. I stare at her. She has the same sad, staring expression as before. I want to take a photo, but my phone's on the bed and I don't want to take my eyes off her. So I lift my hand and wave. She is watching me – I'm sure. Her hand appears, pressed flat against the window and then released. Then she waves at me. It's the briefest movement, but it's definitely a wave.

So many days I have not dared to look out and, when I have had the courage, there is nothing to see. But today, when I have so little hope, I look and I find what I think is only in my dreams — I find the girl, the girl in the window across the road. Kasia. She is looking back at me. She sees me — and all at once I exist. If she can see me then I am real. She waves at me and I am the bravest I have been — I wave back.

I do not dare to stay. The baby cries and I have to go. Now I think, why did I not do more? Why didn't I try to communicate somehow? Maybe she wouldn't have understood — but maybe she would.

Who knows when I will see her again?

Why did I not mouth, 'Help me'?

20

True to my word, I start trying to build up my stamina again. I've been pacing myself, restricting my activities and building up very gradually. I've been using Nav's book, which has given me lots of ideas. I rest it on the bed when I'm reading it, like he suggested – though I would never tell him that! I don't know if it's because of the book, or if I was just ready to start again, but I am definitely making progress.

One of the things I've been doing is walking up and down the road, increasing by just a few steps a day. Now I'm actually sitting in the café down the road, five minutes away from home, telling Ellie all about it.

It was Ellie's idea to meet at the café and it feels amazing – I haven't done anything like this for so long!

Ellie stirs her milkshake with a straw and then looks me straight in the eye. 'Don't kill me, Kasia,' she says.

'Why would I kill you?'

'I did something.' She hesitates.

'Something?'

'I talked to Josh again.'

'What? He spoke to you again, about me?'

'No – this time I spoke to him. He was on his own, standing near the lockers. It seemed like a good opportunity. I couldn't resist!'

'And what happened?' Her sheepish expression is making me nervous. 'Are you going to tell me he's asked *you* out?'

'No, no – of course not! I just . . . I told him about you – how you like him.'

'You didn't!' I am stunned and I feel hot all over. How could she?

'He likes you,' says Ellie. 'I could tell when he asked about you before. He gave this sweet little smile when I said your name. I mean it, Kas – I'm not making it up.'

'What did you say?' I ask. 'What did *he* say?'

'I told him you were well on the road to recovery and that you could walk as far as this café.'

'And?'

'It was a good hint, you see – because then he said,

"Do you think she'd like to meet me there?"'

'What?' I exclaim. 'He really said that? This had better not be a wind-up!'

'I mean it, Kasia. I said you'd meet him here tomorrow at four.'

'OMG!' I don't know whether to be angry with Ellie or not. I *told* her not to say anything to Josh, though I'm kind of glad she did. Only – tomorrow, that's so soon. I'm not sure if I'm ready. What if I wake up tomorrow and don't feel up to it? What if he's put off when he finds out how little I can do? Will I have the energy to wash my hair? And what on earth am I going to wear?

Well, Ellie can help with that one. 'What am I going to wear?' I ask her.

She smiles, looking relieved – I think she was scared I might hit her.

'So you don't mind? You're not angry?'

'I'll take a rain check on that,' I tell her.

'Let's go back to yours and have a look in your wardrobe, see what we can find,' she suggests.

I nod.

Back in my bedroom I lie on the bed while Ellie stands in front of my open wardrobe.

'My jeans press on my legs,' I tell her. 'I wore them for the concert, but they really weren't comfy.'

'Maybe leggings then? How about these? And this top's nice? You can wear a pretty scarf. Hey – I remember when you bought this!'

She pulls out a shimmery pink scarf. I remember too. We were at the local market and Ellie spotted it. I loved it straight away. It feels like a lifetime ago. I want to be that me again.

'Great idea!' I tell her. 'I can't believe I'm going on a date with Josh! Are you sure you're not making this all up, Ellie?'

'You're the storyteller, not me,' Ellie says, laughing. 'But try not to think of it as a date – just a chat in a café. Take it a bit slowly, see how things go.'

When I wake next morning, I can feel my glands pressing on my neck and my jaw aches too. My legs aren't too bad, though, and my head is clear, so I'm pretty certain it's mostly anxiety. I'm going to do this – I'm actually going to meet Josh. I am tempted to skip my usual routine and stay in bed to preserve my energy for later, but I know that's not sensible. I will do everything apart from my walk, as I will walk to the café later.

The day feels so long. I listen to podcasts and an audio book. I do some work for Judy.

'You look nice,' says Mum, when she sees me dressed after lunch.

I wish I'd saved the scarf for later, so it didn't look so obvious that I was making an effort.

'Are you meeting Navin? You made up! I'm so glad...'

'Actually Mum,' I interrupt. 'I'm just meeting a friend in the café. Someone I haven't seen for a while.'

'Well, don't . . .'

'Stay too long,' I finish. 'OK, Mum, I do *know* that. You don't have to tell me.'

'There's no need to be so angry, Kasia. I only want the best for you, that's all.'

I didn't mean to snap at Mum and I feel terrible, seeing the hurt look on her face.

'Sorry, Mum, I just want to be treated like I'm normal for once – not some fragile piece of china. I won't stay more than half an hour, I promise.'

As I walk down the road, I wonder whether it is better to be waiting there for him or if that might look too keen. I don't want to keep him waiting, though.

I am so nervous. In the end I arrive on the dot of four, but Josh isn't here yet. Two minutes go by and I start to panic that he's not coming. And then he walks through the door.

I'm breathing too fast. I try to slow it down. For so long now, I've been a girl who's ill — that has become my identity. It's like I can barely remember the person I used to be — a girl who might meet a boy in a café. Josh is in school uniform. His long hair suits him and his eyes are smiling at me even more than his mouth.

'Hiya,' he says, sitting down opposite. 'Long time no see!'

'Hi,' I say. I smile back.

There's an awkward pause. I've got to say something else but . . . what? I am so relieved when he speaks.

'How's that woman you saved? She OK?'

'Yes.' The word comes out much quieter than I expect. I feel myself blushing. How does he know about Mrs G? Maybe Ellie told him.

'I had a great aunt,' he tells me. 'She died after a stroke. No one found her for three days. I wish she'd had a neighbour like you — to call an ambulance and that. Maybe she'd have been OK.'

'That's sad,' I say.

I can't think what else to say. I've said four words so far altogether. He'll think I can't talk properly if I don't manage a full sentence.

'Do you want a drink, a cake or something?' he asks.

'Thanks – a hot chocolate please.'

He grins. 'That's what I want too. Cream on the top?'

I nod and wait while he goes to order. I wonder if I should offer to pay.

There's a couple in the corner but apart from that the café's empty. I'm glad it isn't full of kids from school.

He sits down with the drinks. I sip mine and feel an instant moustache of cream above my lip. How embarrassing! The cream was a mistake – I should have thought. I wipe my mouth quickly with a napkin.

'It's lovely. Thank you,' I tell him.

He smiles, but he doesn't say anything else. It's down to me. I'm struggling to think of something to say.

'How's orchestra?' I ask. 'I thought the show was great!'

His eyebrows go up. 'Were you there?'

OMG he didn't even notice me. I was sure he had! But then he was busy playing in the concert and chatting to people afterwards – like that Chloe.

'Yeah, I made a big effort to come,' I tell him. 'I overdid it actually.'

I mentally kick myself – why did I bring *that* up?

'I hope you'll be back in the orchestra soon,' he says. 'We're playing Beethoven's Symphony No. 5 this term.'

'Oh, I love that!' I find myself humming it aloud and he grins.

'So you're much better now?' he says. 'I mean, you look fine – you look great. I like the scarf.'

I feel myself blushing as I nod. 'I'm definitely on the mend.'

'Will you be back at school in September?'

'I hope so,' I say. 'That's what I want anyway.'

'A friend of my mum's has ME,' he tells me. 'She's had it for years so I know a bit about it.'

'Really?' I'm not sure if this is a good thing or not. It might make him more understanding but he could also think I might never get better. That's what I worry about. I mean, I know I'm not his girlfriend, but who'd want to go out with someone who's always ill?

'It's good you're getting over it,' he says. 'It's a right bummer getting something like that.'

'It hasn't been easy,' I say.

'So what do you do all day at home?' he asks.

'I have a tutor who comes once a week, so I do some school work,' I say. 'I listen to music, to podcasts and audio books and I sit and look out of the window. Now I'm getting better I go for short walks too.'

God, that must sound so dull!

'Are you up to going to see a film?' he asks.

I meet his eyes. He is actually asking me out – on a date! So many things whirl through my head, but how can I say yes? I can't even cope with TV right now, so how could I sit in the cinema? The brightness of the screen, the flashing movements, loud backing tracks – I can already feel a headache coming on at the thought. But if I say no, he might never ask me again.

'What film?' I ask, playing for time.

'I'll have a look and see what's on,' he says, taking out his phone.

I want to say yes. My heart says yes but my head is panicking.

Josh looks up at me and frowns. 'Are you OK?'

'Yes.' I nod emphatically, trying to shut up the inner voices.

He holds out his phone and points to a film. 'This is out next Friday. Have you heard about it? I really want to see it.'

'Oh – yes, me too. I read a review online.'

And that's true – I really do want to see it. It would have been an easier decision if he'd said a film that I knew I'd hate.

'So – next Friday, then? Is it a date?' he asks, smiling.

A date. He actually said the word. Those eyes – they've dazzled me, sent me crazy because I hear myself answer with the words I know I shouldn't say.

'Yes, that'd be great.'

His smile is worth it, but my head is beginning to feel really thumpy.

'I have to go now,' I tell him. 'But this was nice.'

'Shall I walk you home?' he offers.

'No, that's OK,' I say. I would have liked him to but if Mum sees him I know she'll pound me with questions I'm not yet ready to answer.

'Can I have your number then?' he asks – and I

give it to him. And he gives me his too. I now have Josh's number in my phone.

I stand up and my legs feel wobbly. I have to hold on to the table for a moment.

'Are you sure I can't walk you home?' he says again.

I take deep breaths, hoping desperately that I'm not going to collapse on the floor, then shake my head.

'I stood up a bit quickly,' I tell him. 'I'm fine now.'

I pull my wallet out of my bag.

'It's OK. Put that away,' he says.

'Thanks.'

'See you Friday then,' he says. 'I'll text you.'

'Bye, Josh.'

We walk in opposite directions and I can't resist a quick glance back at him. Did all that really happen?

When I get home, the strength drains from me and I can't face the stairs. I lie on the sofa for a while.

'You haven't overdone it have you, Kasia?' Mum fusses when she finds me later.

'No, I just felt like resting here for a bit,' I lie.

'Good girl,' says Mum.

But I don't know what I'm going to do now. I'm so thrilled that Josh has actually asked me out, but I know the cinema is a bad idea. I've said yes, though, so I've got to go.

Ellie comes round straight after school next day. I've made it downstairs and she's cross-legged beside me on the sofa.

'So – tell me all!' she demands. 'How did it go with Josh?'

'We're going on a date on Friday – to the cinema!' I tell her.

'But you told me you can't even watch telly!'

'I couldn't say no,' I say. 'But I don't know what to do. I'm not really up to it.'

Ellie's smile falters a bit. 'You can't just do stuff because someone else wants you to, you know.'

'I know!' I say. 'But it wasn't that easy. He likes me, I can tell, and I do want to go on a date with him.'

'But you've gone all gooey over him! Don't let your heart rule your head or you'll end up in trouble.'

'I'm not gooey!' I protest. 'I just don't want to mess this up. What do you think I should do? Tell him the truth – that I'm not up to it? I might never hear from him again.'

'But he *has* to know, doesn't he?' Ellie says. 'If

174

you're going on a date with him, you can't just pretend you're OK.'

'I'm getting better all the time,' I remind her. 'I don't want to put him off.'

'So you're going to go to a film even though you don't feel up to it?'

'Shhh,' I say, looking anxiously towards the bedroom door. 'I don't want my mum to hear.'

She lowers her voice. 'You're going to go to a film even though you don't feel up to it and you're not even going to tell your *mum* what you're doing?'

'If I tell her, she won't let me go.'

'This sounds like a bad idea, Kasia.'

'Thanks! Don't forget you set this all up in the first place!'

'Just be careful, that's all I'm saying,' says Ellie.

Her voice softens and she makes me soften too. I don't want to fall out with Ellie like I did Nav – I don't know what I'd do without my best friend.

'I will be careful, Els. If the film is too flashy, I'll just close my eyes and meditate. I'm sure Josh won't notice.'

Ellie laughs.

That night I can't sleep. I'm thinking about Josh and

175

worrying about the cinema. I can't lie still. I get up and sit by the window, drawing the curtain aside so I can look out. There is a light on in the upstairs room opposite. The curtains are closed but they must be thin because I can see a silhouette behind them. Is it the girl? I'm sure it must be.

She seems to be just standing there. Maybe the baby has woken and she is trying to sing him back to sleep. I wish she'd open the curtain and look out. Perhaps she would wave to me again.

As I watch I see another silhouette, taller and broader than the girl. I can't be sure but it could be the woman who lives there. The silhouettes move, blur. It's like watching a shadow puppet play. The arm of the bigger silhouette suddenly swings round and the smaller silhouette drops out of view.

I gasp. What just happened? I can't be sure but it looked as if the woman hit the girl round the head so hard that she fell. Did I really see what I thought I saw? With shadows it's very hard to tell what's happening.

I go back to bed and lie awake for hours.

The baby cried so much today and even I could not soothe him. I cannot keep my eyes open. I sneak to my room to lie down, while they eat downstairs. If I don't lie down I think I will fall. I just want to rest, but I sleep. I did not mean to sleep. I wake with a fright and Auntie is here, screaming. I jump up so fast. The baby is crying again and I did not go to him. Lazy, she calls me. Lazy, good for nothing. How dare I lie down? How dare I ignore the baby when he cries!

I feel so angry. 'I work hard,' I tell her.

'How dare you answer back!' she screams, her mouth opens wide like a lion's as she roars. 'You are nothing! So ungrateful! You forget how lucky you are to have a home here. You go to him — stop him crying right now!' she demands. 'This must not happen again!'

I rush to the baby. I hug him, rock him until he finally sleeps. I am so tired. Too tired.

When I finally can go to bed, I must sleep very deeply because suddenly the light is on and she is yelling again.

'What is wrong with you? Can't you hear him crying? Did you not hear my warning before? You stupid girl!'

I stand quickly, wiping the sleep from my eyes. 'I'm so sorry! I didn't hear!'

Her hand is raised and she shoves me so hard I hit the wall behind.

I go to the baby, but it takes a long time to soothe him back to sleep. When I return to bed I want to sleep, but I cannot. This time it is me that cries.

21

Friday has taken so long to come around. Every hour has seemed to last two – but now it's really here. I am going on a date – a date with Josh. I'm not feeling great, mostly due to lack of sleep and overexcitement, but I am not too bad. Mum and Dad are going out too, for their anniversary. I've convinced Mum that I'm well enough to be left on my own so I don't need to tell any lies about where I'm going. They are going early and I will be back before them. This is clearly meant to be!

Josh texts to say he'll meet me at the bus stop. I hadn't even thought about how we were going to get to the cinema. I haven't been on a bus for months and months. At least the bus stop is so close and has seats, and we can get off right outside the cinema. I decide I will watch out of the window and go down early, as soon as a bus leaves, so I can be sure of getting a seat at the bus stop. Even if have to sit there an extra ten minutes it will be worth it.

When the time comes, I head out, crossing the road carefully. Some people are waiting for a different bus, so there are only two free seats, but I get one of them and sigh with relief.

I feel a nudge as someone sits down beside me. I am astonished to see that it's the woman from across the road – the woman from number forty-eight.

She doesn't speak but surely she recognises me? I think about what I might have seen last night in the window. The woman is sitting here so casually, she looks so ordinary. She couldn't have hit the girl, could she? Maybe it was the man – or maybe it simply didn't happen. I want to say something – to ask about the girl. I try to frame sentences in my mind – something I could say to start a conversation.

'Hi,' I say awkwardly. She turns in surprise.

'Do you remember me?' I ask. 'I live across the road.'

She nods and gives a small rather forced half-smile. Then she looks at the ground. She obviously doesn't want to talk to me, but I carry on talking anyway.

'How's the baby?' I try. 'Is your niece still helping you out?'

'The baby's fine – he's growing fast,' she tells me. 'Getting heavy!' She holds her arms out as if carrying a heavy weight and laughs. 'And my niece is a great help – I'm lucky to have her.'

Now she seems friendly, though I'm sure it's an act. It's so hard to tell. I try to think what else I can say. Do I dare ask again if the girl would like to meet up?

At that moment a bus pulls up and the woman gives me a nod as she stands. Then she turns away and steps on to the bus.

'Hiya! You look like you're in a dream!'

I jolt as Josh sits down beside me in the spot the woman has vacated.

'You OK?' he asks.

'Yeah.' I smile at him and his eyes meet mine. They sparkle in a way that makes my heart flutter. Maybe Ellie's right – I am going gooey.

He looks at his watch. Was I staring back too hard? 'Bus shouldn't be long,' he says.

I'm glad because I'm finding the hard bench uncomfortable. It's hurting the back of my legs and I could really do with my cushion, but it would have been too embarrassing to bring it with me.

When the bus comes, the seats are at least more comfortable, but I had forgotten how jolty a bus can be. The way the bus swings round corners and stops abruptly at junctions makes me ache and feel slightly queasy, and I cling on tight to the pole beside me, while trying to look relaxed and carefree.

'You sure you're OK?' he asks.

'Yeah.' I need to change the subject. 'How's school?' I try.

'S'all right,' he says. 'So much revision, though – it's doing me in. I'm that tired – I can imagine what it's like for you, now!'

'It's not quite the same,' I comment, feeling a flash of irritation. 'It's not like normal tiredness.' I realise I sounded a bit abrupt. I didn't mean to snap at him. 'I'm sure all that studying must be really hard, though,' I add.

'Yes! I'll be so glad when the exams are over. Do you know Ricky and Raj?'

I shake my head. 'What about them?'

'Oh – it's nothing. Not really interesting if you don't know them.'

I'm not sure what else to say. I feel like we're struggling for conversation. Maybe once we get off the bus it will be easier.

'Have you seen any other good films lately?' I ask.

'Not really,' he says. 'The last film I saw wasn't great. Chloe thought it was OK, but . . .'

'Chloe?' I can't help commenting. 'Is she your ex or something?'

'No – we're mates,' he answers.

I feel myself relax a bit. We sit silently and I think maybe this is OK – to be relaxed together and not feel we have to talk all the time.

At last we reach the cinema.

The film isn't bad, though it's a bit violent, and it reminds me of what I saw last night across the road. I wonder again what really happened and I think about the woman at the bus stop – was she being friendly, or was she just pretending to shut me up? Then I feel Josh's fingers reaching for mine. He's holding my hand. His hand is soft and warm and gentle.

But although I'm caught up in the film and loving the feel of Josh's hand in mine, the action scenes are increasing and there are too many flashes and bangs. I start to feel unwell.

'Going to the loo,' I whisper, pulling my hand from his clasp.

The dark of the stairs in contrast to the brightness of the screen makes my head spin and I'm relieved to be out in the corridor. When I reach the loos, I splash my face with water, but I don't feel any better. The glands in my neck are pulsing painfully, my head's thumping and I feel weak and dizzy. I realise I won't be able to go back in. I can't face it. What is Josh going to think?

I stumble back out into the corridor and sit down on the floor, leaning against the wall. I am not sure how much time passes before Josh appears looking worried.

'There you are! I thought you were taking a long time. What's wrong?'

'I'm sorry, Josh.' Tears start sliding feebly down my face. 'I just don't feel all that great. I'll probably be OK in a minute.'

'There's only half an hour to go,' he says. 'Come and watch the end and then I'll take you home. It's only sitting down.'

I shake my head. 'I can't. You go back in if you like. I'll just stay here.'

'Really?'

He looks uncertain, but he's edging back towards

the door to Screen One. I feel another wave of irritation that he would do this instead of looking after me. But I brought this on myself. I should never have agreed to come.

'I don't think there'll be a bus for half an hour, anyway,' he says.

When I look up, I realise that I can't wait even that long.

'Josh, actually, I need to go home now. And I don't feel up to getting the bus.'

'What? Do you want to call your mum to come and get you then? I don't have money for a cab.'

Tears are streaming down my face now. I feel such a fool. 'My mum doesn't know I'm here.'

He raises his eyebrows. 'Why not? Doesn't she like you dating?'

I don't answer.

'Where does she think you are?' he asks.

'At home.'

'So what do you want to do?' he asks.

I'm panicked. I can't think. 'Ellie's house isn't far from here,' I tell him, 'Crown Street. If I can make it there, maybe she'll lend me the money for a cab.'

I'm not actually sure I can even manage the short

walk to Ellie's but I don't want to admit that.

'Sure — I know Crown Street. Here — hold my hand,' he says, helping me up.

We make it to Ellie's and she and her mum fuss over me. Her mum kindly offers to drive me home. I am so grateful. Josh says he hopes I feel better soon but he doesn't say anything about texting me, or seeing me again.

Back at home, I can't face the stairs. I lie on the sofa and suddenly I'm crying and I can't stop. I've messed it up with Josh. I've messed it up completely. It was too soon — I should have waited until I was much better.

And now I've lost him. Why would he want to date a girl who can't even sit through a film without feeling ill? I feel so pathetic, so stupid. I just about make it up to bed before Mum and Dad get back.

I have three days where I'm barely able to move.

'Very strange,' says Mum, 'this sudden relapse out of nowhere. And when you'd been doing so well.'

Josh doesn't text. I feel angry. Maybe he doesn't want to go out with me any more but to not even check how I am isn't nice. Surely he'll call.

Three more days go by and I am still in bed. I'm feeling worse. The whole trip to the cinema was too much – the bus journey, the strobe-like action of the film, the walk back to Ellie's. I can't stand the light now and need the curtains closed all the time or my head starts pounding. I don't even feel like I can sit up. I feel so low – as if I have fallen down a deep, deep well. I am stuck in the dark at the bottom and I can't move. Someone found me and I thought I was going to be rescued, but all they have done is lowered a tube to give me water. I am being kept alive but no one knows how to get me out. What kind of life is this?

I thought I could fight this illness and beat it, but I can't. It always wins. Maybe I am never going to get back to school, never going to be able to have a relationship. If this is my life now, then what's the point? I am not sure if I want to live like this.

Gradually over the next few days I can tolerate light and sit up for a bit. After a few more days I don't feel able to get out of bed but I am able to go online for short spurts. I try to distract myself with the Facebook support group. I write about how depressed I feel about my life, but when I read it back it sounds like I am wallowing in self-pity and I delete it all –

every word.

But later, I try again. I write about what happened with Josh in more of a storytelling style, and when I read it back I'm pleased with it. I've managed to laugh at myself and my lovesick stupidity, which is something. I didn't name him, of course – even though it's a closed group, I wouldn't want anyone knowing all the details.

I decide to post it on the website, but when I check after half an hour, no one has 'liked' it, or commented and I feel a wave of disappointment. Maybe they'd rather compare symptoms than talk about relationships.

But later on I check again and I have three 'likes' and two comments. Dina says, 'Don't be so hard on yourself. You fancied him, so it makes sense that you really wanted to go. I've never had a date with a boy. The only time one asked me, I had to cancel three times, and then he gave up, believing I was giving him the brush-off – even though I tried so hard to explain it was because I wasn't well. I hate letting people down all the time. It is so hard to have a boyfriend when you are like this.'

Mimi says, 'Thank you for cheering me up, Kasia!

I've been having such a bad day and you wrote this in such a funny way it made me laugh and laugh. I can see what a good writer you are!'

I am cheered by these replies, but still sad too. I messed up my one chance and I can't bear it. Josh hasn't texted me at all and I'm not sure whether I should text him after what happened.

Ellie texts me a few times. I tell her not to come over as I really can't face anyone — but she turns up anyway.

'Are you angry with me?' she asks, flopping down in the chair by my bed. 'I never meant this to happen. I was only trying to help.'

'I know, Ells,' I assure her. 'Of course I don't blame you. I should have been honest with Josh about the film. We could have done something else instead.'

'So when do you think you'll see him again?'

I shake my head. 'I won't. He hasn't texted or anything.'

'No way!' says Ellie. 'He seems so nice!'

'I can't really blame him,' I say, sighing. 'I know it's hard for people to understand because I look OK — they can't tell how ill I feel.'

'You still want to see him?' Ellie asks.

I shrug. 'It doesn't matter, does it? He clearly doesn't want to see me. I think it's over, Els.' Tears start to roll down my cheeks and I can't stop them. 'I want to feel special and close to someone and loved – you know? And I want to go to school. I want a normal life.'

'Yes, I know,' says Ellie, giving me a gentle hug. 'But maybe forget about him for a while. Let's just try and get you better first.'

22

Even though nothing has really changed, Ellie's words have cheered me up, and so have the responses on the Facebook group. Today I feel like sitting and looking out of the window for the first time in days. There is nothing to see at the house across the road. The curtains upstairs are closed. I turn to the bus stop, and watch the people for a while. I think about the woman from forty-eight, sitting next to me there and wonder what she's doing today.

I walk to my parents' bedroom so I can look out the back. I am kind of hoping Nav will be there, in the garden next door – and he is. He's planting something in a flower bed. The garden is looking beautiful now, in the sunshine. It's full of flowers.

Maybe today I'll try to go downstairs. I'd love to sit outside with Nav and watch him gardening, and chat like we used to. Why am I so stupid? Why was I so mean to him? I wonder whether I should try texting him again.

Then I see that Mrs Gayatri is sitting out there – on the chair that I used to use. I'm pleased for her, glad she feels well enough – but I'm disappointed too. Nav has company already.

I go back to bed instead. I will forget about boys and concentrate on my studying. I open a file and try to write answers to some history questions. I have to do enough work so that they will let me stay with my year group and do my GCSEs next year.

When Judy comes she is impressed with the work I've done.

'I want to get back to school in September – even part-time or something,' I tell her. 'I want to do my GCSEs.'

I see the immediate doubt in Judy's frown. 'Kasia, I think you have to be realistic about it. I also hope you'll get back to school part-time in September, but I still think you'll have to start with the year below, and cut the number of subjects you're taking too.'

I can't answer. I can't speak. This is not what I want to hear.

'Kasia?'

I have to prove her wrong. I must.

I am getting better and better, and I'm feeling more positive too. I begin to go downstairs and move around the house again, and it's not too long before I decide to go out for my first walk in ages. I stand on the front doorstep and let the sunshine warm my face, and breathe in the fresh air. I look across the road at number forty-eight. I wonder about ringing the bell again. It's such a lovely day – warm and sunny but not too hot – even if she's a few years old than me, maybe I could convince the shy girl to come out for a short walk – to the café perhaps. It's so long since I've seen her – but she did wave to me that once.

I decide to take the risk. I ring the bell. The woman comes to the door. She looks at me suspiciously.

'I've just come to ask after your niece,' I tell her. 'It's such a nice day – I wondered if she'd like to come to the café with me. She could bring the baby too.'

'My niece is fine. She is busy and not in need of company, as I told you before,' the woman says. Then, as if worried she has spoken too sharply, she adds, 'It is kind of you to ask, though.'

'Doesn't she ever want to come outside?' I press.

'Of course she does. But not today.' And she closes the door abruptly.

There's nothing more I can do.

Over the next few weeks I focus on increasing my walking and studying, determined to go back to school in September. The first time I manage a fifteen-minute walk I feel amazing! It's the most I've walked in nearly a year – a whole year. I am managing more studying too.

One day I see Mrs G, who is putting a bag of rubbish in her wheelie bin. We are very happy to see each other.

'Off anywhere nice?' she asks.

'Just up and down the street. I'm trying to build up my steps,' I tell her.

'Why don't you go to the park?' Mrs Gayatri suggests. 'You know – the one on Alwyn Road? Wouldn't that be nicer than walking in the street?'

'That's a good idea,' I say, nodding. 'I couldn't get that far before but I think I could now. It would be a change of scene. I haven't been there for years.'

'I haven't been there for many years either,' says Mrs G. 'I used to push Devi there in her pram.'

The park is a little more than ten minutes away, but I make it there – through the park gate and on to bench. I hope I will be OK to walk back again. Sitting there, I feel a sense of calm as I look across the grass to the pond, watching the gently rippling water, the trees rustling. I can hear the road but it is a gentle hum in the distance – the birdsong of the park fills the air. Two ducks glide across the water, hopeful for food. I feel a tiny thrill inside to have walked this far. Mrs G is right – it's so much nicer than the street.

I sit breathing calmly and enjoying just being here, watching the passers-by. There's a man pushing a buggy. Then a girl comes. She's pushing a buggy too. She approaches the pond and pulls out a bag of bread crusts. The ducks change direction, instantly heading towards her. The girl reaches into the bag of bread. There's a sign up saying, 'Please don't feed bread to the ducks', but she doesn't seem to have noticed. I wonder if I ought to say something, but I don't want to interfere.

She has long dark hair swept back in an untidy ponytail. She's wearing a thin top and a skirt that doesn't seem to fit her properly. There's something familiar about her. My heart skips a beat as I catch sight of her face. It can't be . . . can it? She's the girl I've seen in the window – the girl from number forty-eight. But how can it be her? The grey buggy is familiar — it's like the one I've seen the woman from forty-eight pushing a couple of times. It must be her.

I watch intently as she feeds the ducks, talking to the baby. It is so weird to see her outside — in the park, after all this time. She looks OK — perfectly normal. I've had all these crazy thoughts about her and now here she is, at the park, looking fine. I want to speak to her. I hope she might turn this way and see me. Maybe she'll recognise me too. But she's looking only at the baby and the ducks. She gives the baby a crust and I see his arm try to throw but the bread lands next to the buggy. The girl bends to pick it up and throws it herself.

I stand up and meander towards her, trying to look as if I'm just wandering over to take a look at the pond. I stand a metre or so away. Now I'm up close, I can see that she's definitely not Farah, the girl from the missing persons website. Her face is a similar shape but her eyes and mouth are different.

The baby turns and looks at me with curious eyes.

'Hi,' I say to the girl. 'Cute baby.'

The girl tenses. She keeps looking straight ahead at the pond, clutching the bag of bread crusts tightly as if she thinks I want to steal them. It was a friendly comment, but I feel like she is radiating fear. Something must be very wrong for her to react this way.

The baby giggles at me. 'Bababa,' he says, pointing at the ducks.

'Ducks?' I say to him. 'You like feeding the ducks?' He grins.

The girl takes another crust from the bag and throws it. She's still acting as if I'm not there.

'Do you recognise me?' I ask gently. 'I've seen you in the window. I live across the road. I've never seen you outside before. I wondered if you were OK? I'm not being nosy or anything. I just . . . are you OK?'

I'm babbling. She isn't answering.

'Do you speak English?' I ask, suddenly wondering if she's understood a word I said.

She grabs the handles of the buggy and walks quickly away towards the gate.

'Sorry,' I call after her. 'I didn't mean to upset you. I was only . . .' But she's through the gate and gone before I can finish my sentence.

'See — I am kind. I will let you go out. Don't speak to anyone.' That's what she told me today. It is so long since I've been anywhere — I can barely believe what she says.

She told me the way to the park, and to come straight back. I am happy to be alone here with the baby and the birds — to enjoy the air that smells of pine cones and to feel the sun on my back. If I speak, bad things will happen.

Then the girl approaches. What does she want? Who is she? Then I realise I know this girl. She is Kasia from across the road. Her voice is kind and gentle. I want to talk — to tell her — but I don't have the words. And I am too scared. I want her to go, to leave me alone. But she keeps talking and I can't understand much she says.

I must leave before I find my words because they might come out — and that is dangerous, too dangerous. I walk quickly, the bag of bread still in my hand.

Kasia can't see me now. The hunger gnaws at my stomach. I stand by a tree. There is no one in sight. The motion of *walking has sent the baby to sleep. I pull a crust from the bag, hard and rough, a tinge of blue. It is repulsive, but I have not eaten since yesterday, and then just scraps. The bread still smells of bread. My stomach aches for it. I stuff it into my mouth. Then more, one crust after another until it's gone. Then I go back to the house.*

23

When I get home, I sit in my room by the window, wondering why the girl hurried off so quickly. Maybe I shouldn't have spoken to her. I think I frightened her with all my questions.

I feel so tired now, but I'm pleased I managed the walk to the park. I'll go there tomorrow, as long as I feel up to it. Maybe the girl will be there again – or maybe she'll look out of the window tonight.

When Judy comes in the afternoon, she's impressed by the amount of work I've done. But when she tries to teach me, I can't concentrate at all.

'Kasia, if you carry on like this I worry that you won't manage to do even one GCSE next year, let alone ten. I know how much you want to achieve that, but your health has to come first. You mustn't overstretch yourself.'

I bite my lip. 'Maybe you're right and that's not realistic.'

Judy's face lights up. 'Finally!'

'Maybe I could just do six — or seven.'

'I'll tell you a secret,' she says, leaning towards me. 'I only have five GCSEs myself. I failed the other three. I was devastated at the time — but I was still able to do A levels and become a teacher. It hasn't held me back in any way. And taking fewer subjects and doing them a year later will also not hold you back in life.'

'You might be right,' I grudgingly admit.

'You need to listen to your body and pace yourself. You can study at any time in your life — you don't have to stick to some government schedule. You have to do what's right for you.'

It's evening but still light when I glance out of the window and suddenly she's there — the girl in the window opposite. She's looking straight at me. Does she recognise me from the park? I hope so. Perhaps she doesn't understand English — maybe that's why she seemed so scared earlier, she didn't realise I was the girl who'd waved to her.

She's still staring at me. I'm sure she realises it was me. How can I tell her I just want to know if she's OK? If she needs help, I want to help her.

I try to mouth the words 'Are you OK?' But then she's gone.

A few days later I make it back to the park. The sun is bright again, smiling down on me warmly, and I feel positive. I believe I will get better. One day my life will get back to normal and this illness will be something I simply look back on as a bad memory.

The park is busier today than when I came last. The warmer weather has brought more people out of the shadows. It is particularly popular with people who have babies. I look out hopefully for the girl with the buggy, but I don't see her.

My phone vibrates. There's a message from Marek. I open it eagerly.

'Guess where I am?' he asks.

My heart thuds. Has he come back? Is he at home? 'Where?'

The next message is a photo. It's a front door. It looks vaguely familiar, but it isn't ours.

Then another photo — a smiling face. This I do recognise. It's my Aunt Maria in Poland.

'Lodz!' I reply.

'Yes — I'm home,' he tells me.

'This is home – HERE,' I message. 'Not Poland.'

'It feels like home,' he responds. 'At least I am with family who welcome me with open arms. It's nice to see our cousins. I'm going to stay a while and work with Uncle Andrzej.'

'Dad is not going to be pleased,' I respond.

'Dad is never pleased,' Marek replies.

And I'm right. Dad is mortified. He switches immediately into overdramatic mode.

'It's a complete humiliation,' he tells Mum, thumping the table so hard that a teaspoon jumps in the air. 'I told them so many times how much better life is here – the opportunities there are for our children. Now my good-for-nothing son goes crawling back begging for work in your brother's bakery – sweeping the floor! It's a disgrace! How they'll be laughing.'

'He's a little lost, our Marek,' says Mum, a wistful look in her eyes. 'He will find his way in time.'

'Lost! After all the guidance we have given him!'

I cannot bear to hear them arguing, so I go to lie down on my bed.

As I lie staring at the ceiling, a memory floats into my head. It's a hot day, years ago. We are lying on the grass side by side in the park, the one on Alwyn Road.

Mum is sitting on a bench somewhere near, chatting with a friend.

'What do you want to do when you grow up?' I ask Marek.

'I don't know,' he says.

'A footballer?' I ask.

'I love football but I'm not good enough,' he tells me. 'What about you, Kas? You're clever. You could do anything.'

'An author, or a musician, or a doctor, or a scientist, maybe,' I reply.

'Wow! That's a lot of ideas! Whatever you do, you must use that amazing brain of yours.'

'You have a brain too,' I say. 'There are so many different jobs – I don't know how anyone decides what to do.'

'You don't have to decide yet,' he tells me. 'We don't have to decide for years and years and years. There's plenty of time.'

I am watching TV with the baby. It is CBeebies — which is very good for learning English. I feel like a normal person, sitting on sofa. I have never sat here before. Watching TV — this is my reward — because I work hard. She says it's good for the baby to watch.

She says, 'See, you are good and things are better for you. You take the baby to the park and now watch TV. You have a good life, we are kind to you. Yes?'

I nod. I hope I am allowed to go the park again soon. My stomach rumbles. On TV some teddies are eating cake.

24

Today in the park I am stunned to see the girl straight away. There she is by the pond again, whispering affectionately to the baby in the buggy, who stares up at her with his big round eyes. I stop still, staring, my heart beating fast. This feels so important. I don't want to frighten her but I am determined to speak to her again – and this time I don't want her to run away.

She hasn't seen me yet. I walk slowly closer until I see her shoulders tense. She glances round at me.

'Please don't run off,' I say to her. 'I don't want to scare you. I only want to talk. I want to know that you are OK.'

She shuffles nervously and I think she is going to leave. I need to keep talking to her. I need to make her stay.

'I hardly ever see you outside the house,' I continue. 'You're always inside.'

'You also,' she whispers, glancing up at me and then back towards the pond.

My heart is racing. She's speaking to me – she *does* understand, though she has a strong accent.

'Yes, I've been ill,' I tell her. 'And you? Is it the same for you? Are you ill?'

'Ill?' she repeats as if unsure what it means.

'Sick, not well, poorly,' I try.

She shakes her head. 'I not sick,' she says.

'So why don't you go outside?' I ask.

'I am here – outside,' she says, still barely audible, a puzzled look on her face.

'But you hardly ever come out, do you?'

'Yes, many days inside,' she says, nodding. 'Lots of work.'

'School work?' I ask.

She shakes her head. 'No school for me. Baby, house – lots of work. You not go school,' she comments. 'You home many times too.'

'I'm not well enough to go to school,' I tell her. 'How old are you?'

She doesn't answer.

'What's your name?'

She's gone quiet and I'm not sure what to say. I want to ask her about the woman dragged into the car, whether she saw – but she's not answering questions about her name or her age so I don't want to press her.

'Are you really OK? Do you need help?' I ask.

'Help? How you help? You want care for this baby?'

I have a sudden thought. 'Is he yours? Is that why you're not at school?'

'My baby? No! But I care for him much.'

'You shouldn't have to care for him all the time, though,' I tell her. 'You should get days off. Are you happy?'

I see her eyes darken for a moment. She isn't. I'm sure she isn't. Her whole posture, her bent shoulders, her scared eyes say she's not.

'Happy?' She shrugs. 'My life not so bad. I love baby.'

'He's really cute.' I smile.

She nods. 'Now I must go.'

I'm frustrated. I'm sure she's not telling me everything.

'Can you meet me here again?' I ask her. 'I just want to be your friend.'

'Friend is good.' She gives me the briefest smile back.

'Tomorrow?' I ask. 'Can you come tomorrow?'

She shakes her head.

'Friday?'

'I try,' she says, and she walks quickly away.

I am afraid.

I spoke to the girl — to Kasia. She spoke to me. She is kind, but I broke the rule. Speak to no one. Will they know? Do they have eyes everywhere? Do they watch? Will I be punished?

When I get back from the park, I hear a voice. There is someone here. Someone different. It's a girl and she's crying. He calls me and I run upstairs. I must always run to him when he calls.

'That girl in there,' he barks, 'she is sick. You will nurse her. Make sure she takes this medicine. You understand?'

I nod meekly. 'Does she need food?' I dare to ask.

His glare makes me instantly regret my words. 'You think I'm an idiot? You think I will give you food for her so that you can scoff the lot? Your aunt will see to her food. You give her water and medicine and tell Auntie if she gets any worse. She must get better quickly and return to work. I am losing money.'

Then he looks at me and I don't like it. It is as if he can see through my clothes and it makes me shudder inside.

'You could always be her replacement,' he says, his voice low and full of threat. 'If I had my way you would be there already, but your auntie likes you. She says you are good with the baby. She wants you here to work in the house. But if that girl does not recover soon, I will have it my way. Don't you forget that.'

He's gone. I am not stupid. I know what he means. I know what work this girl does. My life is bad, but not like that.

I cautiously open the door. She is older than me by three or four years. She lies sobbing on a mattress the same as mine. There is no sheet, no cover. She wears only shorts and a T-shirt, her long matchstick legs have clear bruises. She is shaking, I think with cold – but as I get nearer I can feel the heat coming from her. She has a fever, not chill.

I speak my own tongue to her, but she does not respond. She may be too ill or maybe she doesn't understand.

'I have medicine for you,' I tell her. 'A tablet to take with water. You must take it and you will feel better.'

'For what?' I hear her whisper. She does speak my tongue after all.

I don't have the answer to this. 'You want to die?' I ask.

'I care not if I live or die,' she says.

211

'If you live there can be hope for something better to happen. If you die there is no chance, no hope,' I reply.

'Something better. You think there is something better? There is not. There is nothing. This is it.'

Her voice is quiet but bitter, desolate. She makes me afraid. I cannot lose hope like this girl has. I need to believe in the better. I must.

She slowly sits up and takes the tablet with a sip of water. Then she turns away from me and lies back down.

She is here for four days, but she does not speak to me again. Then her fever has gone. Then so has she.

The other girl recovered but now I have her fever. I realise they brought her here to stop other girls catching it, – and they wanted me to tend to her so they didn't catch it themselves. I know now how bad the girl felt.

Auntie tries to insist that I do my chores, but she sees that I cannot. She says as I am ill she will be kind and let me rest. She gives me the tablet and the water, but no food. She says best not to eat if I am ill. But my body has no strength to fight this illness – I am so weak with lack of food, I think I will surely die.

I wish I'd told the girl, Kasia, my name so someone knows I was a person once – a person with a name, someone who lived.

I am too hot and then so cold I shake — and then too hot again. I dream of scraps — of mouldy bread meant for birds. I cannot even dream of proper food now. It is so long since I had some.

She keeps me away from the baby — she does not want him to catch this fever. He is my warmth, my consolation, and I miss him. I know he cries for me and she cannot soothe him.

25

Next time Ellie comes to visit I tell her all about meeting the girl in the park.

'So what the woman told you could be true,' she says when I finish.

I nod. 'The girl does go out and she is looking after the baby, but she didn't answer when I asked how old she is. No way does she look eighteen and she seemed scared about something. I've still got a bad feeling about it.'

'Maybe I could come with you at the weekend?' Ellie suggests. 'See if she's there?'

'Yes please!' I tell her.

I go to the park on Friday and I sit on the bench for ages, but the girl doesn't come. I watch from the window in the evening, but I don't see her then either. Ellie comes with me on Saturday, but there is still no sign of her. Ellie seems as disappointed as I am. I go alone on Sunday, feeling less hopeful. In the distance

I see a girl with a buggy, but as she gets nearer I see that it isn't her.

She said she wanted to be friends. Why hasn't she come back?

I keep watching for the girl all week, but I don't see her. On Friday I walk to the park but there's no sign of her.

I'm almost back at my house when I suddenly see the girl coming towards me with her buggy, clearly on her way to the park. I was too early! I'm so excited I start walking quickly towards her, wishing Ellie was with me. But when the girl sees me she stops suddenly and turns to look behind her, as if afraid that someone might be watching or following.

'Hi! I've been hoping to see you!' I call. 'Are you OK?'

'Yes. OK.' She speaks quietly, looking down at the pavement – not meeting my eyes. She may be saying she's OK, but she doesn't sound it. Her eyes are flickering anxiously and her fingers are clutching the handle of the buggy tightly.

'I went to the park a few times but you didn't come,' I tell her.

'Please – you must go,' she tells me. 'I must not

speak with you here.'

'Why not?' I ask. 'What's wrong?'

She looks towards the house, as if she's scared someone will see.

'Surely they won't mind you speaking to me?' I say.

She shrugs. I can see her shoulders shaking.

'What are you frightened of?' I ask gently. 'Are you in danger? If you are, tell me and I can call the police for you.'

'Please! No! No police! Go. Please go!' she manoeuvres the buggy around me.

'Wait!' I beg, but she walks off quickly before I can stop her.

I want to go after her but my legs won't let me. The walk to the park and back is as much as I can manage.

I am well again. I'm looking after the baby once more. I was taking him to the park — so happy to breath fresh air. But the girl, Kasia, she was there, in the street — too close to the house. She wanted to speak to me — but I was so afraid they might see. I went quickly. I hoped no one saw me speak to her. The park was peaceful. Baby and I, we were happy there.

But when I return, Auntie is yelling and screaming about the nosy girl from across the road. She saw us. Why did Kasia come so close? Why can't she leave me alone? She puts me in danger — she knows nothing. She thinks she can help, but she can't. She can only make things worse.

Things are worse. Auntie told him and he says I must go — and I know where he means. He's going to send me to work in the other place, where the sick girl came from.

She protests — she doesn't want me to go and they are arguing. I know who will win. She is bad, but he is the boss. She has gone shopping and taken the baby with her. She has been out for over half an hour.

'Come,' he says. 'Get in the car now.'

'Where are you taking me?' I ask in terror.

'You'll know soon enough — and you won't be coming back here.'

'Should I pack clothes?' I ask, trying to delay. I have a skirt, two pairs of jeans and two tops, some ragged underclothes — that is it.

'You won't be needing them,' he says.

His words freeze my blood. Is he taking me to the other place — or is he planning to kill me?

I get in the car, but she comes back and starts shouting at him. She wants me for the house and the baby. He is angry that she is making a scene. I look up in the window opposite. I wish the girl, Kasia, was looking out now — was witnessing this. If he takes me, I will disappear like a wisp of smoke. Kasia will never know where I've gone.

Now she is in the car — and the baby too. They keep shouting at each other as he drives. We turn into a road and he slows down at a house. I know in my heart this is it. This is where that other girl lives and more girls too. This is where most of the girls they bring for better life, jobs, education in this country — this is where they end up. I am the lucky one — or I was.

He has the car door open and is beckoning me out.

*'I have a better idea,' she tells him. 'Sort out that girl —
that nosy parker girl. Teach her a lesson. She's the cause of
trouble — not this one. This one I need. The baby needs.'*

*The baby has started to wail, as if he knows what is
happening.*

'Shut him up, can't you?' he demands.

But she can't.

*'Let me,' I say, and I touch the baby's hand — speak soft
words. His big eyes look at me, his face striped with tears. But
the screams turn to sobs. At last he smiles and then closes his
eyes.*

*They are both quiet. My fear floods out to fill the uneasy
silence.*

*'OK, have it your way,' he tells her. 'A little accident,
perhaps? I will enjoy teaching that no-good girl a lesson.'*

*He gets back into the car and turns it round, and we are
driving away again. I look at the sleeping baby and stroke
his dark mop of hair. I tell him in my head how he saved me.
He saved me.*

*I am to be saved — but what about the girl across the
road? What about Kasia?*

26

It's Mum's forty-fourth birthday. Dad suggests we have
a BBQ lunch. Mum invites Devi who is vegetarian, so
Dad gets some veggie burgers. She asks Mrs G and
Nav too, but Mrs G isn't up to it – she's finding the
hot weather hard to cope with. Nav can't come either
– says he's *busy*. Dad is taking the kitchen chairs and
folding table out into a shady spot in the back yard.

Ellie texts me while I'm sitting in the kitchen.
I've told her about seeing the girl. She wants to know
what I'm going to do. I text back, 'I'm not sure'.

Dad picks up another chair from the kitchen
and we follow him outside. 'Nothing from that
godforsaken son?' he says to Mum. 'He couldn't even
be bothered to send his mother a card. That's what he
thinks of us. You are deluded, Anya, if you think he
cares an ounce.'

Mum shrugs. I know she's disappointed not to
hear from Marek. I'm surprised he hasn't even sent

an eCard or a WhatsApp message.

Devi arrives which is a relief as Dad stops going on about Marek and instead starts talking to Devi about her online business. She sells bags and accessories online and is making a small but decent living doing it.

My phone buzzes. 'Maybe you should call the police,' Ellie's texted.

'I don't know,' I reply. 'She was so definite that I shouldn't involve them. I want her to trust me. She's free to go out, so it's not like she's a prisoner.'

'I think she wanted to talk, just not there – not so close to the house,' I text next. 'Are you free later? Let's go to the park again. Maybe she'll come.'

Put your phone away, Kasia!' Dad demands. 'It's very rude.'

'Sorry.' I put my phone on the table. It vibrates immediately but Dad is still watching so I don't pick it up.

'I've been telling Anya she should do the same with her cakes,' Devi says, still talking about her business. 'She is a superb baker as we all know.'

She points to the birthday cake – a lemon sponge with cream that Mum has made.

'You could, Mum!' I tell her. 'You could totally

run a cake business!'

'It's in her family,' Dad comments. 'But I'm not sure Anya would know where to start. How do you sell cakes online? You can't just put them in the post!'

'You'd have to market yourself on local websites, and that kind of thing,' Devi explains to Mum. 'Then there'd be a lot of word of mouth. I'll help you if you're interested?'

'It would be a dream to do that,' Mum says, nodding. 'To spend my days baking and have people paying for my cakes! And if I can work here, I can care for Kasia too. But I can't see it as a reality.'

'You should try, Mum,' I say. 'What have you got to lose?'

'I'll think about it,' Mum agrees. She reaches for a knife to cut the cake.

'Wait!' Devi exclaims. 'Where's the birthday candle? Surely we must sing and you must make a wish as you cut.'

'I'm too old for all that,' Mum protests.

'No, you're not,' I tell her.

I'm not sure if we have any birthday candles, but I go inside, search the drawer and find one. Then I have another hunt for some matches.

Dad is getting impatient.

'Can't we just eat the damn cake!' he calls.

'Patience, patience,' Devi teases.

At last the candle is lit and we all sing, Dad imitating an opera singer and making us all laugh.

'A triumph,' he declares, as he tastes the cake.

The house is stiflingly hot. I want to see Kasia. I need to warn her that she is in danger.

'It's so hot in this house, shall I take baby to the park?' I ask.

'No — you are not going out today,' she says firmly. 'You are right it is hot. I will open some windows.'

She comes with a key and opens the narrow top windows. The tiny key glints as she turns it — as if it is speaking to me. Where does she keep this key? If I could find it, could I escape? Could I go and warn Kasia? Would I dare?

She puts the key in her pocket. I have no chance of retrieving it there.

I sit on the sofa and hug the baby, snuggling up as we watch cartoons. He wriggles away — he is too hot for hugs and the high open windows are letting in only more hot air. But I need the comfort. I am afraid — afraid for Kasia. They want to stop her interference — teach her a lesson.

I want to push the door open and beg and plead with

him — tell him to take me to the other house, but not to hurt the 'nosy girl'. But if he knows I am eavesdropping I will be punished — locked in the basement as he has done once before. And if he decides Kasia should have a little accident, it will happen and I cannot stop it.

If I am quiet, maybe there is something I can do. I go back to my room and look out of the window, across the road. I hope to see her — to see a light on in her room, to warn her somehow — but her house is in darkness.

27

The next morning a parcel arrives from Poland. I recognise Marek's writing straight away.

'Marek didn't forget!' I tell Mum. 'It's just a day late.'

Mum smiles and opens it eagerly. She gasps when she sees what he's sent. It's an old scrappy-looking hardback notebook. She opens it and I can see it is full of writing, in Polish.

Mum holds it to her nose which seems a weird thing to do with a book. Then she hugs it close to her chest and tears prick her eyes.

'It's my mother's,' she whispers. 'All my mother's wonderful cake recipes are in here. I've tried to reinvent them from memory, but here are the real recipes. Where on earth did Marek find it?'

She eagerly opens the accompanying letter.

'Aunt Maria found this at the back of a cupboard and I thought you might like it,' Mum reads Marek's words aloud. 'She said she never uses it. I'm sending it to you for your birthday.'

'Something he didn't have to pay for – how is that a proper gift?' Dad asks Mum.

Mum shakes her head firmly, and begins to leaf through the book. 'Marck knows this book means more to me than hundreds of pounds – and now I have it, maybe I will do as Devi suggests. It is a sign! These are the most amazing recipes. It is a precious, precious gift, Stefan.'

Dad tuts, but he doesn't argue.

'Now, which shall I make first?' Mum mutters, flicking through.

'I don't know!' I tell her. 'I'll leave you to decide – I'm off for my walk. See you soon.'

He is going out in the car. I can see the expression on his face as he kisses her goodbye. What can I do? While she is in the kitchen I dare to search their bedroom for the window key. This is a huge risk and my heart is pounding with fear as I search. But I cannot find it. I do find something — an empty notebook with a pen attached. I could write a note — but how could I get it to her? It is such a short distance, but I have no way to get a note to the house across the road. I tear a page carefully from the notebook and take the pen — just in case — and on my mattress, I sit and write the note. I am not used to writing in English, but I try.

If she looks out of the window I could hold it up but she would be too far away to read it. If I stand on a chair I could push it out of the top window. If she was watching, she would see that I was trying to send her a message and come outside and pick it up. But maybe she is safer to stay inside — where he cannot get her. I stand by the window, the note tucked in my jeans pocket.

Then I see Kasia's front door open. She's coming out —
and I pull the note from my pocket, wave it in the window,
hoping the flash of white paper will catch her eye. But she
does not look up. She is walking away down the road. Maybe
she goes to the park in search of me. But she does not turn
right. She is going to the shops or somewhere else. She is out
in the street and in danger.

Maybe I am wrong. Maybe his threat was a pretence.
Would he really do something so bad? I stay here, in the
window, waiting for her to return, waiting and waiting even
though I should be cleaning the floors. I want to see her come
back safe.

Then I hear a door bang and see across the road that the
boy who lives next door to Kasia has come out. I wave the
note once more. He glances up and sees me! I hold up the
note, press my nose against the window, my mouth making
the shape of 'Help' over and over, though my voice stays
silent. I dare not call.

He looks puzzled. I stand on the chair — quickly, before
he turns and walks away, I push the note out through the
small window. He is watching! He is still watching as it
flutters over the bins near the front step. He hurries across
— searching for the note on the ground. He is so close to the
step.

I hold my breath.

He has the note! He walks away from the house as he reads it. Then he starts to run.

28

The weather is still hot today and I feel sticky, but I'm glad to be outside where at least there is a slight breeze. I was going to go to the park but it's too much effort to walk in this heat and I decide to go to the café where there is air conditioning. I'm happy that I can do this now – choose to walk to one place or another. And I am walking a little further each week too, without feeling worse.

The café is busy today and I can't get my usual table by the window. I manage to find a space with a partial view of the street. I sit and have a cooling pineapple juice and watch the people going past along the pavement. Everyone seems to be in a rush today. Being still so much of the time has made me realise just how much time people spend hurrying around, with never a chance to think. I have plenty of time to think – maybe too much.

Then I see someone familiar. It's Nav – walking

past, like he's on a mission. He's wearing denim shorts and a dark green T-shirt that suits him. He pauses, taking a step back and glancing in at the window – looking at my usual table. Could he be looking for me? Probably not, though I wish he was. I wish he'd turn and see me, but he doesn't. Seeing him this close makes me ache for his friendship. I decide I need to try one more time to make amends – maybe he'll respond if I see him face to face.

I hastily gulp down the rest of my drink and head to the door. In my rush I knock a cup on the next table and some coffee spills over the top. By the time I've apologised and am out of the door, I can't see Nav at all.

The street seems eerily quiet now. It's weird how that happens sometimes – one minute there are so many people and cars, and a few moments later, no one.

I start to walk towards home and then I hear a voice calling my name. Nav. Is it Nav? As I turn to see, a car screeches behind me. I look back sharply to see it swerving – on to the pavement! Silver metal is coming right at me. I step back in horror, trip, can't get my balance, and the car's still coming.

From behind, someone pushes me sideways so hard I go flying. And then I'm on the ground, I feel the sting as my hand scrapes the concrete. There's a scream, a thud and a surge of exhaust fumes that burns my throat as a roaring noise hits my ear. Then silence.

I dare to open my eyes, try to lift my head, but my vision is fuzzy for a moment and by the time I can see, the car is a speck in the distance. I'm lying on the pavement. To one side of me I can see bare legs, brown skin. Someone is lying close to me, still – too still. I lift my head to see denim shorts, a green top, a familiar tousle of dark hair. Nav.

'Nav!' I yell. 'Nav! Are you OK?'

I'm scared. He seems so still. I try to sit up, relieved to find I can move, and crawl nearer.

'Nav! Nav!'

Then my view is blocked. A woman is standing over me, and I see another kneeling by Nav. 'What happened? Are you OK?'

'A car,' I croak, 'did you see? It mounted the pavement. Nav – he must have seen it. He pushed me out of the way and I think it hit him.'

'You just lie still. I'm calling an ambulance,' she tells me.

But I'm trying to sit up. 'Nav! Nav!' I cry. 'He isn't moving!'

'Please lie still,' she says. 'My friend's a first-aider. She's checking him out.'

So I lie there, not moving – and we wait. A crowd gathers but there's no one I know. I've no sense of how much time passes – it feels like some kind of weird dream. The ambulance comes. The paramedic checks me over and helps me to stand. I am relieved to find that I can. I have cuts and grazes, bruises, but I am OK.

'I saw what happened,' I hear someone say. 'It was going straight for the girl. That boy leapt in and pushed her out the way.'

They have a blanket. They're putting it over Nav. Is he dead? Are they going to cover his head?

'Nav!' I yell.

'Hey, hey – he's unconscious,' says the paramedic.

'Will he be OK?'

'Let's just get you both to hospital,' she says firmly. I want you to be checked over thoroughly and then the police are going to want to talk to you.'

I hadn't noticed the police until now, standing back talking to the other paramedic.

I don't think I need to get looked over, I feel fine, but I don't argue as I want to go with Nav in the ambulance. I struggle with the seat belt as Nav is strapped to the stretcher. I pull out my mobile to call Mum as the ambulance starts up and I tell her to tell Devi.

Mums gasps and swears in Polish. 'I'll be there as quickly as I can,' she tells me.

I watch Nav all the way to the hospital. He doesn't move or wake up, and when we arrive he is whisked away. My legs give way as I try to stand, so they bring a wheelchair for me. I'm sure my legs aren't injured, but they are throbbing and I know I can't walk another step today.

I am left in a bay with a curtain, still trying to process what happened. Hit and run. That's what it was – deliberate – the driver came straight for me. But why?

Mum is in tears when she arrives and I tell her what happened. I am checked out – and have to explain about my ME when the doctor wonders why I am finding it hard to stand. They say I can go home, but I want to wait, to find out if Nav is OK.

'Devi will keep us informed,' Mum tells me. 'Let's get you home.'

A policeman asks me questions before we go – not that I can tell him much. The car was silver. It came straight at me. That's all I know.

I tell the policeman about the silver car I saw out of the window that time, the man who seemed to drag the woman into it. But he says that silver is a very popular colour for cars and it's not likely to be connected. Of course, they never found any proof of an abduction so it's not really any help.

It feels like hours before Devi calls to say that Nav has woken up. He has severely bruised ribs and concussion, they're not sure how bad, but he can't remember anything about what happened.

'They're keeping him overnight,' Devi tells me, 'just as a precaution, because of his head. All being well he should be able to come home tomorrow. I told him what I know and he's asking for you. Demanding to see you!' she says. 'I didn't know you two had made up.'

'We hadn't, but he saved me,' I reply. 'He saved my life. Can I come and see him?'

'Tomorrow,' says Devi. 'Wait until he's home. I think it's best for you both to rest today. You and Nav have been through a terrible ordeal,' she says. 'I hope the police manage to track that car down and get that idiot off the road.'

'Yes,' I say. 'I hope Nav is OK. Tell him I'll see him tomorrow.'

29

The next day I feel a bit battered after being flung to the ground, but I'm relieved that apart from that I don't feel too bad. As I get dressed mid-morning, I hear a car and look out to see Nav getting out and walking awkwardly up the path with Devi. I want to go next door straight away but Mum insists I give him an hour or so to settle back home.

Later on, Mrs G lets me in. 'Are you OK, Kasia?' she asks. 'I am so shocked by what happened – so relieved that you and Nav are both alive and not badly hurt. Nav is in the garden – you can go to him.'

'Surely he's not gardening?' I ask.

'No – resting outside and admiring his handiwork. The garden really is looking lovely.'

Nav is sitting on a plastic chair, facing the garden. He turns his head slightly and grins as I am come outside. It's that old familiar Nav smile from before and it warms my heart to see it. I realise just how much

I've missed him. Devi said he couldn't remember what had happened with the car, and I wonder for a moment whether he's also forgotten what I said to him – how I upset him. I'd be glad if he had forgotten that.

'You've transformed it,' I say, sitting down beside him and waving my arm towards the flowerbeds.

'Not bad, is it?' He beams. 'Needs a lot of water in this heat, though. Pity Nani doesn't have a sprinkler system.'

'Oh, Nav – you saved my life! Thank you!' I can't help blurting out.

'S'all right,' he says, looking a bit embarrassed.

'You were nearly killed,' I say. 'It was very brave.'

'It's all a blur,' he tells me. 'I don't even remember where I was going.'

'That car coming at me – it's another weird thing,' I say, 'like the girl across the road. She's real, you know? I spoke to her.'

'The girl across the road,' he repeats, looking puzzled.

'You remember I told you about her – and we knocked at the door but no one answered? I kept seeing her in the window but she never came out

– and then I saw her at the park. The people there, they say she's their niece, helping out with the baby and she's eighteen, but she always looks terrified and I'm certain she's much younger than that. I've been worried about her all this time,' I tell him.

'That girl . . . My brain's trying to tell me something,' he says, rubbing his head. 'It's a memory – something to do with yesterday, to do with that girl. I'm trying to think – I'm sure it's important but I can't remember . . .'

'Did you see her?' I ask him. 'She sometimes looks out of the window. You saw her once, remember – you told me.'

'The window?' he repeats. 'The window.'

I can see he's thinking hard. I want to press him – I'm desperate for him to remember. But I try to be patient. I look at the flowers, listen to a bird singing.

'It's no good,' he tells me. 'I'm sure it has nothing to do with that car that came for us, anyway.'

Devi sticks her head out of the kitchen door. 'Just putting your clothes from yesterday in the wash, Nav – I found this in your trouser pocket. There's something written on it – I don't know if it's important? Anyway – here it is, in case you want it.'

Nav takes the piece of lined paper and examines it. 'I'm not sure what this is,' he says shrugging. 'It doesn't look like my writing.'

He pauses, then looks up suddenly. 'Hang on, I remember!' he says. 'Kasia, it's coming back to me. It wasn't me who saved you, it was the girl – the girl at number forty-eight!'

'What do you mean?' I ask, wondering if his head injury might be more serious than anyone thinks. He isn't making sense.

'I came out to go to the shops for Nani,' he tells me. 'I was about to cross the road when I heard a tapping sound, and it was the girl at number forty-eight, at the window. She was mouthing something frantically but I couldn't work out what. Then she dropped a piece of paper out of the window – and it was this note.'

He gives it to me. I read it, feeling goosebumps break out all over me as I see what it says. 'Kasia – you in danger. They want hurt you.'

'How did she know? I don't understand,' I say, partly to myself and partly to Nav. 'How did she know it was going to happen?'

'What you told me about the girl – have you

done anything that could have made the couple there suspicious?'

'No – well . . . yes, maybe,' I admit. 'I've asked the woman about her a few times – and when I spoke to the girl near the house, she hurried off as if she was scared of being seen. Maybe they *did* see.'

'Perhaps they were worried about what she may have told you. They wanted to shut you up,' says Nav. 'The girl must have heard what they were planning.'

'And she scribbled that note,' I say, 'and threw it out.'

'I know I panicked when I read it,' says Nav. 'I'd seen you go out, and I just ran up and down the road looking for you. When I finally saw you, it was almost too late. I was only just in time. I only got to you because she warned me.'

'You both saved me,' I say, shuddering.

'There must be something seriously wrong in that house,' says Nav.

'I've been saying that all along,' I tell him. 'It wasn't the man's car though.'

'Maybe he got a mate to do it,' says Nav. 'His car would have been too obvious. We should call the police. It was attempted murder!'

'But she said no police. She was terrified. They're dangerous people, aren't they? We've seen that today. We need to be very careful. If we speak to the police we may make things worse for her.'

I turn the crumpled paper in my hand, staring down at her words. Then I see on the other side, she has written in tiny writing: 'help me please'.

'Look,' I whisper. 'She does want help. She's asking us.'

'Show me.' Nav takes the paper and peers at the writing.

'We have to do something,' I tell him. 'She got a message to us – now we need to get one to her.'

It did not work. I tried and I failed — I failed so badly. Now two people are harmed, maybe dead. That poor boy — I sent him into danger. What was I thinking? I heard the car, the screech, I looked out — and I saw, far along the road, the two on the ground. That poor girl Kasia. Is she dead? I could look no more.

I am panicked. I cannot stay here with these mad people who will kill a girl in the street for trying to be friends with me — for caring. I must leave.

She is out. I am alone with baby. I put their clothes in the washing machine. This is what she was wearing yesterday — I saw her put the window key in her pocket. I feel for it frantically, but it is not there.

The washing machine whirrs and I go upstairs, taking baby with me. I will search once more for the window key. It must be somewhere. I know she has the front door key with her, but I believe the window key is here in the house. I must be brave. I search their room — every corner, every container.

I think it is nowhere. But then I find it. The tiny silver key glints at me from a small clay pot, a pot shared with pennies and paperclips. This is it. This must be it. I can open a window and I can go – I can leave.

I feel an urgency – I should not wait. But I cannot leave the baby here alone. I will have to take him with me. But no – he is not mine to take! She does not deserve him. She does not care for him as I do. He is safer with me. He will want to be with me. Then I must get not just myself, but the baby out of the window – and I will need the buggy too.

I must move fast – carrying him will be slow and difficult. They could come back at any time. I put baby on the floor, where he kicks his legs and watches me. I turn the key in the front downstairs window. It turns. It clicks. Now I could open it – I could open the window wide and be out.

But where would I go? Kasia, the girl, she is maybe dead or in hospital. Where can I go? I have no one, nothing. They will find me and bring me back – punish me.

Baby has started to cry. I turn the key once more, locking the window. I put the key back in the pot, beneath the pennies. I sit on the floor hugging the baby and as I sob, he puts his chubby arms around me.

30

Nav and I wait the next day for the man and woman to go out. We are next door and Nav is watching from his window but being careful not to be visible. The man goes first at half-past eight, but the woman is still there at 10 a.m.

'It's just our luck,' I tell Nav, 'I bet she'll stay indoors all day.'

But then the door opens and she finally leaves, taking the baby with her. She locks the door behind her. The girl is alone.

'I think she's locked her in,' says Nav. 'If she can't open the door what can we do?'

We go anyway. I ring the bell. No one comes. I lift the letterbox and call through. 'Is anyone there?'

We wait. I call again.

'She's not coming,' I tell Nav.

But then suddenly my view of the empty hallway is blocked and two frightened eyes meet mine the other side of the letterbox – so suddenly and so close that I jump back in alarm. The letterbox snaps shut.

It's the girl. She's really there. I lift the letterbox tentatively again.

'We've come to help you,' I tell her. 'Can you open the door?'

'You are alive!' she whispers, sounding surprised.

'Yes,' I tell her. 'We're OK. Thank you, thank you for your note – for trying to help me. Can you open the door?'

'No. Door locked.' Her whisper sounds so far away, even though I know she's only on the other side of the wood.

'What about the back door?' I ask. 'Is there any way you can get out?'

'Window,' she says, so softly I have to strain to hear. Then she speaks more. 'I find key for window.'

'You'll have to be quick,' I say, hoping it won't take too long.

'I can find – I get it,' she tells me. 'I get key now.'

She disappears and we watch the windows in the front room.

When she doesn't appear instantly I wonder if she's changed her mind and isn't going to come – but then she's there, her face appearing behind the net curtain, her hand reaching out to the window lock, the tiny key between her fingers.

'Quickly, come on. We'll help you out,' Nav tells her.

I look round, anxiously. There's no one in sight. She's opened the window but she isn't moving. I see tears prick her eyes. She is too scared.

'It'll be OK,' I tell her, though I have no idea if it will.

'You have to be quick. Someone might come back.'

'Come on!' I say. 'Hurry!'

Nav holds out his arm and the girl hesitates, but then she clambers out. She leans on Nav and I see that her hands are shaking violently.

He takes her hand, tries to lead her towards the road, but she's not moving.

'This is no good,' she says. 'They will find me. They will hurt me. I must stay. I must go back.'

'No – come with us. We will help you, I promise,' I say. 'Come across the road to my house. It is only a few steps.'

The girl's eyes widen with fear. 'Not safe,' she says. 'They will look near here for me. They know you.

I must go far.'

'Look – there's a bus coming,' says Nav. 'Let's just get on that. At least we'll be away from here.'

On the bus I sit by the window and the girl sits, head down, beside me. She flinches as the bus moves off and so do I, but I know her pain is different from mine. I glance at her, sitting next to me. We've rescued her. We got her out.

'I want to thank you,' I tell her.

She looks at me wide-eyed.

'Your note – you told Nav I was in danger. He saved me. That car would have hit me if it wasn't for you.'

'I hear what they plan for you – "no-good girl" they call you. I think you are good girl. I know you try help. I want help you.'

'Well, you did,' I say, nodding.

'What's your name?' Nav asks gently.

'Reema.'

'How old are you?' I try next.

'Fourteen. Fourteen. Is truth.'

'We believe you,' I tell her.

'And what about your aunt and uncle?'

'They not real aunt, uncle. Not my family.

They tell you lies.'

'What do you mean? Who are they then?'

'The man is friend of my uncle – my real uncle. He tell my uncle they bring me here for good life and good school. They say I help a little with baby and house, but when I come they lock me in there – I cannot go out. No school. No money. Work all day, clean house, look after baby, cook all food for them. Before I come they say no cost to bring me here, but now they say I must work to pay for my journey.'

'That's terrible!' Nav exclaims. 'You've been trafficked! We must get you to the police. They will help you and lock up those people.'

'No police!' the girl shouts, and other people on the bus turn to stare.

'Take me back,' she demands. 'I must go back.' She stands up as the bus pulls to a halt and Nav has to hold on to her arm to stop her getting off.

'Are you all right, dear?' an elderly woman asks gently. 'Is that boy hurting you?'

The girl doesn't answer, but she shakes her head. The bus doors close and she sits back down, hiding her head in her hands.

'I must go back,' she whispers. 'The baby – he

needs me. And the police — they will lock me up too, or they send me back, and my uncle — he not want me.'

The bus stops again and suddenly she's up and running out of the doors.

'No — wait!' I call, and Nav and I jump off too, following as fast as we can.

31

I can't run – the pain is intense and my legs give way after a few steps. I'm not sure Nav should be running either, with his injuries, but he does. We can't lose her now. I stop and stand, panting, watching Nav. He is shorter than the girl but she runs awkwardly and he is faster. He runs past her, turns to face her and blocks her from passing.

Her shoulders are shaking as she sobs. I drag my legs, walking fast, determined to catch up. Nav is trying to calm her down.

'Please – don't cry,' I tell her. 'We want to help you. What do you want us to do?'

'Take me back – you must. Take me back. Now. Now. Now.'

'OK,' says Nav. 'If that's really what you want.'

I open my mouth to protest. After all this – we've got her out and now we're going to take her back? But we can't force her to come. And if we don't take her back, she's going to run off and maybe we'll never find her. Who knows what would happen to her then?

'Come on,' says Nav. 'We can cross the road and take the bus back. If that's what you want.'

She nods and I see her shoulders sink down with relief. I hold out my hand and she grips it as we cross the road. She continues to grip my hand as we wait for the bus. She keeps looking down the road, waiting to see the bus and she's clearly getting anxious.

'Ten minutes,' I say. 'It should be here in ten minutes.'

We wait in silence. I can't believe we're doing this. There must be another way.

'We want to help you,' I tell her. 'Why do you want to go back? Isn't there something we can do?'

'You kind, very kind,' she says. 'I know you kind. I see you at window – I think, kind girl. But no one can help me. It is not possible.'

I meet Nav's eyes, hoping he will have an idea – something to suggest that will reassure her.

A man walks past eating a burger and the girl's eyes follow him intently. I hadn't noticed how thin she was until this moment.

'Are you hungry?' I ask.

'Hungry always,' she says. 'Not much food – only, how you say? What they is left.'

'Their leftovers?' I ask, horrified.

She nods. 'Very small,' she says.

'I'll get you something,' Nav tells her. 'Look – we can go into McDonalds, over there. I'll get you a burger, like that man?'

Her eyes are wide. 'I . . .' She is almost salivating. 'I eat and then you take me back – yes?'

'Yes,' says Nav, though he gives me a meaningful look. He's hoping, like I am, that we'll manage to persuade her to do no such thing. He turns to me. 'You want anything?'

'No, I'm all right. Maybe get her a drink too?'

We find a table at the back of the room. She's breathing fast and everytime someone comes in through the door, she looks round anxiously. They couldn't find us here, could they? I want to say something calming, but I'm not sure what.

'I remember when I first saw you in the window,' I tell her. 'It's so long ago.'

'I remember I see you,' she replies. 'I think you work like me – I never see you come out.'

'The first time I saw you, I don't know if you

254

noticed me at all,' I say. 'Something happened – out in the street. Do you remember? Did you see it? A woman was dragged into a car.'

Reema's face seems to freeze. There's new fear in her eyes. 'You see that?'

I nod. 'I called the police – I told them to talk to you too, but those people you were living with, they said there was no one else in the house, like you didn't exist. I think the police thought I was making it up.'

Reema frowns. I've been speaking too fast and I don't think she's following.

'The police didn't believe me,' I tell her, slowing down my speech. 'And no woman was reported missing or anything.'

'She one of *his* girls,' Reema says, covering her eyes momentarily with her hand.

'What do you mean? Whose girls? Are you saying you know her?'

'She run away from him, from the place – how you say? The no-good place where girls wait for men. They took her back.'

'What? She's a prostitute? Is that what you mean?' I ask.

Reema nods. 'He has place not far where you live.

He bring girls there. They think go school or jobs, but he bring them there and lock them. I lucky one. She wants me – for house and baby. If not, I go there too – for men.'

'But Reema – how can you think of going back when you know all this?' I demand, in horror. 'When you are out and free and you could help those girls?'

'You not understand. These people – they strong, clever, so much power, you know? No one listen me. I speak to police – they kill me. They will find a way.'

'But what about those girls who are forced to be prostitutes, like the one the man dragged into the car?'

Reema closes her eyes tight and then opens them again. 'I cannot help them. I must help for myself. Maybe I tell police and they get sent back to their countries. Maybe they angry – they safer, better life here.'

'Doing that though?' I say, in horror. 'How can their lives be worse?'

'You know nothing,' she says, shaking her head.

'You have to tell the police,' I tell her.

Reema begins to cry.

I'm scared for a moment that she's going to run off

again and I won't be able to stop her, but Nav appears with a burger and a Coke.

While Reema is eating ravenously, I tell Nav what she's just told me. 'It must have been the same car – the one that got that girl and the one that tried to hit me. We have to do something!'

He looks horrified. 'Let's try online,' he suggests. 'There must be an organisation or something that can help.'

We both get out our phones. I explain to Reema that we are looking for someone to help her.

My search for 'trafficked children' brings up Childline. I click the link.

'Here – look, it actually says Childline help trafficked children!' I say, showing Nav. 'It's on the NSPCC website. There's loads about it. I wish I'd seen it before.'

'Why don't you call Childline now?' he says – 'and let Reema talk to them.'

I nod. I turn to Reema and explain about Childline. 'They're not the police,' I tell her.

She looks very unsure, but she doesn't say no. As I begin to tap the number into my phone she doesn't protest. I pray that I will get through quickly, and I do.

I explain the situation and I'm put through to a woman called Megan who listens carefully, encouraging me to talk and speaking back with a gentle, soothing voice.

'Would Reema like to speak to me herself?' she asks.

I hand the phone to Reema and she takes it. I can see her hand shaking as she presses it to her ear. Reema answers questions with one word initially, but then begins to say more. Finally, she hands the phone back to me.

'Kasia, can you tell me where you are?' Megan asks.

I tell her.

'Wait there,' she tells me, 'and I'll speak to social services and arrange for a social worker to come and meet you and Reema. She has agreed that I can tell the police too.'

32

When the social worker, Amanda, and a policewoman arrive, we are all taken to the police station. Mum and Devi have been called and are on their way. Reema asks for me to stay with her while she is questioned but Amanda explains that isn't allowed. She gently convinces Reema that she will be there to support her, and the interpreter speaks to Reema and seems to reassure her. She goes off with them while I wait with Nav in another room. The policewoman asks us questions and we tell her everything.

'To be brought to this country and treated like a slave,' I say to the policewoman, 'it's so shocking.'

'What will happen to her?' Nav asks.

'If she wants to go home we will arrange that. But if she wants to stay here we will help her to apply for asylum. In the meantime, social services will try to find a foster family to look after her.'

'Maybe she could stay with us?' I suggest. 'I can

ask my parents.'

'That's sweet of you, but I think she'll need to go somewhere far from here. Otherwise associates of the people who took her might threaten her and make her go back with them. And people have to go through all kinds of checks and training to become foster parents.'

'Can we stay in touch – will you let us know what happens to her?' I ask.

'I can't make promises about that, but I will try,' she says. 'If you want to write to Reema I'll make sure your letters are passed on.'

We are left to wait for what feels like hours, but probably isn't. Nav plays on his phone.

At last, the policewoman brings Reema to say goodbye.

Reema still looks frightened. She doesn't speak.

'I hope you'll be OK,' I tell her.

She nods.

'Don't worry – you're safe now,' Amanda tells her.

Standing there, Reema looks thinner than ever, even more like the ghost I once thought her to be.

'I'll write to you,' I say.

She doesn't seem able to speak. She says goodbye only with her eyes and then she follows the social worker out through the doors.

Devi brought Mum to the police station and she drives us all back home, as we tell the whole story over again. I am suddenly overcome by weakness and exhaustion. 'I need to lie down,' I tell Mum, as the car pulls up outside our house.

'I'll leave you to rest,' says Nav and he disappears quickly inside Mrs G's house. He seems so keen to leave that I feel a surge of disappointment. I thought we'd become friends again, but maybe I was wrong. The front door closes and I wish I'd said something – said sorry for the way I treated him. But the moment has passed.

I let Mum hold my arm as I struggle up the stairs and sink down on to my bed. It's been an extraordinary day, though I know that something good has happened because of it and that Reema is now safe. But I can't help feeling sad about Nav.

The next day I lie in bed, reading the NSPCC pages about child trafficking. The stories are shocking. Children brought to this country and used as prostitutes or slaves. I read accounts about different children who've been trafficked. There's even someone like Reema — a girl trafficked for domestic service and just locked in the house all the time.

Ellie comes round. We've been texting of course, but she is bursting with questions. I show her the stuff online about trafficking.

'That's incredible,' she tells me. 'I'd never have imagined something like that. You were so right to be suspicious! And you're talking to Nav again?'

I nod. 'He saved my life.'

'I'm glad you've made up,' she says.

'I'm not sure we've actually made up,' I admit. 'I need to apologise properly. I was vile to him after the concert. I don't think he's forgiven me. And I really like him, Ellie.'

She looks at me. 'You mean — you *like* like him?'

I nod, suddenly realising it's true. I can feel my cheeks going hot.

'He's a good guy,' she says. 'You'll have to speak to him.'

I nod again.

Ellie glances at her watch. 'I've got to go,' she tells me.

'Where are you off too in such a hurry?' I ask.

It's Ellie's turn to blush.

'Do you have a boyfriend?' I ask eagerly. 'Here I am telling you about Nav! What aren't you telling me, Els?'

'I have got a date, as it happens,' Ellie says, but there's something weird about the way she's saying it.

'Who with? Come on, spill!'

But Ellie is quiet, not meeting my eyes, picking anxiously at her cuticles.

'There's something I need to tell you and it's difficult,' she says.

I can't think what she's getting at. I joke, 'It's not Josh, is it?'

It's meant to be a joke, but she doesn't smile. 'Oh, God, it's NOT is it?' I say. I don't want Josh any more, but this feels a bit weird.

'It's not Josh,' Ellie says. 'It's Lia.'

'What? You mean . . .'

'Yes,' says Ellie. 'She's my girlfriend.'

This is a total shock. 'But you went out with Callum! I thought you liked boys. How are you suddenly gay? Or bi? Or what? And I didn't know Lia was gay either!'

'I don't know what I am, exactly, Kas. We just

know we have feelings for each other – something more than friendship. I've never felt like this about any boy. But I'm scared. I don't want to be defined as anything. I just want to be myself.'

She's crying now and I feel awful.

'I'm sorry,' I say softly. 'I had no idea. I wish you could have talked to me. You've been so supportive to me and all the time you had this going on in your head. And I haven't even asked you if you're OK, or what's going on with you!'

'I didn't want to bother you with it on top of everything else,' she says, squeezing my hand. 'I'm glad I've told you now, though.'

'So am I. And maybe it's weird but I've been a bit jealous of Lia – thinking she was going to be your new bestie. I feel much less jealous now I know she's your girlfriend!'

'I'm frightened, Kas,' she tells me. 'Scared it will all go wrong. And people are so insensitive, wanting to put labels on things.'

'I'm sorry *I* did that,' I say. 'What does Lia think?'

'She says we both want it, so we have to go for it.'

'And that *is* what you want too?'

Ellie nods.

'Then go for it. Be brave. It probably won't last forever — that's what you told me, didn't you? How many people marry someone they were at school with?'

'You're right — we need to lighten up, just enjoy it. I'm glad I told you   I was scared. I thought it might be too weird for you. I didn't want to lose you, Kas.'

'No chance!' I tell her — and we hug.

I am so happy when Nav texts the following day to see if he can come over. I don't feel up to getting out of bed, but I manage to sit up.

'Can you believe it?' I ask him.

Nav nods. 'We did the right thing, Kasia. I'm glad we did it. I only wish we'd done it before.'

'I hope she'll be OK now,' I say. 'I hope she can claim asylum or something.'

We sit silently for a few moments but it's not an awkward silence.

'Are you OK?' he asks. 'You're back in bed . . .'

'I think it's the shock of everything,' I tell him. 'But I get over setbacks much quicker now. The strict pacing has really helped. I'm sure I'll be OK. In fact, I bet I'll be up and about tomorrow.'

265

Nav nods again. Is that relief in his eyes? Like he cares — really cares? Or am I imagining it?

'I heard you were going out with someone?' Nav asks.

'What? I'm not . . . Oh, Josh? We only . . . we had two dates. It's over now.'

'Good!'

I laugh. I'm sure I see a glimmer of a smile from him. Is he really pleased that Josh is off the scene? Does he actually like me . . . like that?

'Nav?' I say.

'What?'

'I'm sorry for how I was after the concert — for the things I said to you. I was feeling really bad but I know that's no excuse. I didn't mean them — I promise you.'

He says nothing for a moment. Maybe I judged this wrong. I'm asking too much.

'I got the message,' he tells me. There's a brusque tone to his voice. 'I know you're not interested in me like that. I know I'm too short for you — I get it. I never really expected anything more, but I was hurt.'

'Short?' I repeat. 'What do you mean? This was nothing to do with you being short.'

He shakes his head firmly. 'Oh, but it was — even

if it was subconscious, Kasia. No girl wants to go out with a boy who is shorter than her. That's just the way it is.'

'That's rubbish, Nav! Maybe some girls think like that but not me. I could say the same, why would anyone want to go out with someone with ME?'

'I don't care about that,' he says with a shrug. 'I like you. I like you as a person.'

'I feel the same about you,' I tell him. 'Your height was never an issue.'

There's silence for a moment. Somehow we can't look at each other.

'Nav – I really am sorry about the things I said,' I say next. 'I'd enjoyed the party so much and I'd felt so normal – and best of all was being there with you. I was so disappointed when I relapsed, especially as it was two days later. That often happens but it still feels like a kick in the teeth. I'd felt like I was starting to get back to the way I was before – that I might be able to go back to school soon – and then I was so much worse and Dad was so angry too. I lashed out at you. I didn't mean what I said and I'm sorry, truly sorry. Can you forgive me?'

'It's not easy, Kasia. You hurt me big time. I can't

make any promises.'

'Oh – OK,' I whisper.

I'm trying not to cry. I mustn't cry. I mustn't let him see how much it matters.

But then I see he's smiling. 'But if my height really doesn't bother you then I think we should give it a try, if you want to – go out with me, that is? Or even "stay in" with me, when you're not up to going out. Whatever . . . That is the convenience of living next door to each other!'

'I'd like that,' I say softly. 'Yes please.'

33

Mum shows me an article in the newspaper saying six young women, believed to have been trafficked to this country for prostitution against their will, have been rescued. Three men have been arrested, including a man who, along with his wife, has also been charged with keeping a fourteen-year-old girl as a domestic slave. I can't help wondering about the baby. Where is he now?

'We're so proud of you, *moje kochanie*,' Dad tells me. 'What happened to those young women was terrible and you saved them.'

The house across the road is empty. I don't know how long it will be before new people move in.

The couple at forty-three have got engaged. We only know this because Devi has done a far better job of getting to know our neighbours than we ever did. They are having an engagement party, and they need someone to make the cake. Devi has recommended

Mum. Mum is terrified. She said no initially but Devi has convinced her to do it – she says they want a very simple design and are more interested in a cake that tastes good.

Devi then insists that she get some business cards printed to hand out. 'This is the way word spreads,' she assures Mum.

Mum is in the kitchen for hours. She won't let anyone come in. Then, at last, she calls me.

'Do you think it's OK?' she asks, doubtfully. 'I had to use online tutorials to learn how to make the flowers.'

'Mum!' I exclaim, looking at the white cake, decorated with lemon-yellow flowers and a gold band. 'It's beautiful! They will be so happy!'

Mum smiles. 'I didn't think I could do it. Just shows you what you can do if you try.'

'And with the right encouragement,' I remind her. 'You wouldn't have even tried if Devi hadn't pushed you.'

'True,' Mum admits. 'That Devi is a one. I think I need to do a proper course – food hygiene and professional baking, or even a business course.'

'I could have a look online – see if I can find one,'

I tell her, 'when I'm back from my walk.'

'That's kind. Thank you.'

But when I come out of the house, I have another idea and decide to walk to the library. The librarian directs me to the folder of information about local courses. I find exactly what Mum is looking for at the local college. My eye is also drawn to a leaflet in a rack, from the NSPCC. They run Childline and it makes me think straight away about Reema. I must write to her. I've heard nothing about how or where she is.

The leaflet is about an open gardens scheme. I pick it up. The NSPCC have a scheme where people open their own gardens to the public for a day and members of the public pay to go in. The money goes to the NSPCC. I think immediately about Mrs G's garden. Nav has done wonders with it. Would Mrs G let him open it to the public? It would be amazing to raise money for the charity that has helped Reema!

I take the leaflet and knock next door on my way back, eager to show Nav.

'This looks great! I want to do it!' he tells me. This is no surprise – I knew he'd love to show off the garden. 'Do you think anyone will come, though? I mean, people round here . . .'

'Let's call and find out what you have to do first,' I say.

He phones straight away but comes off the phone looking disappointed. 'It's too late to get into the programme for this year,' he tells me. 'Maybe next year. I'll have that garden looking even better by then. And you'll be fitter too – and able to help me!'

'It's a shame,' I tell him. I'd been so excited about the idea and I don't want to wait a whole year. 'Couldn't we do it anyway, just arrange it ourselves? We could still raise money for the NSPCC.'

'How would people know to come?' Nav asks doubtfully.

'We could put flyers through all the doors down the road,' I say. 'We can offer tea and cake too – Mum could bake the cakes. I bet people would come.'

'Maybe you could play the cello, too!' Nav suggests.

'I'm not sure – I haven't played for so long. But I could try . . .' I tell him.

'If Nani and Mum agree then, yes, let's do it!' Nav says, smiling. 'It can be a practice run and we can try to get in the main programme next year.'

I write to Reema. I tell her about the plan to open Nav's garden. I'm not sure how interested she'll be. I wonder if she'll even want to hear from me. Perhaps it will just remind her of the horrible time she had here. I tell her how my health is improving, how I am able to walk further and am planning to go back to school in September, starting with two mornings a week and building up slowly.

I send the letter to Amanda, the social worker, so she can forward it to Reema wherever she is. I'd love to get a reply but I don't hold out much hope.

Two weeks later, a letter arrives for me.

'*To Kasia,*

How you are? I am good. I so happy you write with me! I stay with nice family and Amanda help me find one cousin I know living in this country. I see my cousin now – he very happy to see me. I go school soon. People helping me so I can stay in this country.

You save me. Without you I still be in that house, and only look at you from window, with bad life. No life. I still scared someone find me – lock me again. But I am far away.

273

Thank to you Kasia and your friend Nav. You good people.
I hope you happy life. Maybe I meet with you one day?
Reema'

I show Nav. 'I'd love to see her again one day,' I tell him.

We work together on the flyer for the open garden. Mum is very enthusiastic and is busy baking cakes and putting them in the freezer. When the day comes, the weather is glorious – hot and sunny with a gentle breeze. I am standing in Mrs G's garden, though I will sit down soon as I still get pain in my legs. I have to be careful but I've built up my strength so that I can now walk for fifteen minutes twice a day.

I know now that I can't control this illness, I can't fight it or beat it with positive thinking – even though it really helps to have a positive attitude. I have the best chance if I pace myself carefully, but I can't always predict how things will affect me.

I am enjoying being in this flower-filled haven, listening to people admiring what Nav has done. Lots of people are here, walking around Mrs Gayatri's garden. She is sitting proudly at a table, taking money as people come through the gate – money that is going to the NSPCC, to help children like Reema.

We didn't know whether people would actually come. But they have! Kath and John from forty-three have come, the engaged couple who now want Mum to make their wedding cake next year. From down the road, a family we'd never met, Helene and Birou and their three young children have come. I can see Mrs Gayatri has her eye on them, afraid they will tread on the flowers, but they are perfectly behaved and far more interested in the cakes.

Ellie's back from her holiday in Spain, and she's here with Lia sitting on the new bench. They both look very happy. I can also see several people I recognise from the café. Dad is chatting to a man I don't know, and Nav is telling a pair of older ladies the names of some unusual plants. I think I hear someone ask if he will do their garden. He meets my eyes and smiles.

'So nice,' Mrs Gayatri says softly. 'I didn't think people in this road would come.'

'But they have,' I say. 'They have.'

'Maybe we make a friendlier street now — better neighbours,' she says.

I nod.

'And you have done so much,' she comments.

'This.' She sweeps her arm round the garden. 'And that girl across the road. These are big achievements. You have made a difference to the world – even from your sick-bed.'

I smile.

'And my Nav, I'm glad you are friends again – maybe more than friends?' There's a twinkle in her eye.

'Do you mind . . . me not being Hindu?' I ask anxiously.

'No, I don't,' she says. 'I disapproved of Devi's boyfriend all those years ago not just because he wasn't Hindu but because I thought he was bad for her. And so it proved – he didn't stick around. But I lost my Devi for far too long. I have learnt my lesson. I will let my Nav make his own choices – and I know you are a lovely girl.'

'Hey – how about some music?' Nav asks. 'I've brought your cello out on to the patio.'

I've had a practise and I know I can't play for long but I manage a few tunes and it is wonderful to be playing again. People stop chatting and gather round, listening. I enjoy the applause.

I am tired after the garden open day and have a day in bed. I post pictures of the garden on the ME Facebook page and explain about fundraising for the NSPCC. I get lots of 'likes'. I also write about Reema – but I do it as a story, without writing her real name. I say it really happened, though.

Dina replies, saying both these things are amazing achievements – especially for someone with ME, who is often housebound. She says it just shows what is possible – and she reminds me how I thought my life was worth nothing when things went wrong with Josh. 'Life is not only about boyfriends and exams,' she comments. 'You make me realise that many things – even tiny things – can make our lives worthwhile. What you have done is not small, though. You have done something incredible for someone else.'

I am relieved that, after a day in bed, I feel OK and am up and about again. My phone rings and it's Amanda. She's happy for me to meet up with Reema.

'We can't bring her anywhere near you,' Amanda explains. 'There may still be people around who'd recognise her. She may not be safe. Sometimes trafficked girls are so brainwashed that they run off to be with the people who held them captive. They think they are safer that way – and they fear the authorities here more.'

'That's terrible,' I say. 'I hope Reema wouldn't do that.'

'Are you well enough to travel?' Amanda asks.

'How far?'

'Maybe an hour on a train,' she says. 'I could meet you the other end.'

'I think so,' I tell her. 'I'll have to talk to my mum. Can Nav come too?'

Mum is worried, but with some persuasion agrees that I can go. Nav says he can't come as he's taken on too many gardening jobs for neighbours and anyway, he thinks it is right that I am the one to meet Reema. I enjoy the journey so much. Every little thing that I couldn't do when I was ill I appreciate now in a different way. Simple things like travelling on a train. Mum is hoping by this Christmas that I will be well enough for a trip to Poland.

Amanda meets me at the station and drives me to a café. I spot Reema immediately. She jumps up, looking so happy to see me. She's wearing smart jeans and a pretty top, and she has a healthy glow. She seems relaxed, not stiff and terrified anymore. After a quick chat, Amanda says she'll leave us for half an hour and come back.

'You look great,' I tell Reema, when she's gone.

'You too – your health better now?'

'Up and down, but right now definitely getting better,' I say.

'I meet many good people,' she tells me. 'They help me much. I miss baby. I worry for him but they say he has foster family too – nice people. I still scared sometime – alone, in dark, or loud voices – but I go to school September. That is everything for me.'

'That's good.' I smile. 'Your English is getting better, too.'

'I want learn – very much,' she says. 'My foster mother very nice. She help me. And my cousin too. Long time I wait for this.'

I nod. 'I wish I'd been able to help you sooner. All that time . . . Do you want to tell me your story, how you ended up there? I mean – I want to hear, but only if you want to tell me . . .'

'I tell you, Kasia. You my friend – but my English still not so good.

'When I eight year old my mother very ill. My dad work hard but he also ill and we have very little money. He go to work in another place far away. When my mum die one year ago, my uncle take my brothers to live with him but he not have much money. He say he has good plan for me – his friend will bring me England for good life. I go school and also help family with baby. They will pay me good money I can send back to help my brothers. So I come here. I love the baby, I cook good food – but they not pay me, no school, locks on doors, much, much work in house. They say I am nothing. It is terrible life. I not eat with them, but wait they finish and I must stand eat in kitchen. They not let me sit.'

'That's awful,' I tell her. 'What a terrible thing to do – they completely deceived you.'

'I lucky maybe.' She shrugs. 'It is better I care for baby and not for men. Some girls not so lucky.'

'But you saved those girls too!' I remind her.

'I hope they happy,' Reema says, nodding. 'You visit me again?' she asks.

'Yes – if you like, I'd love to keep in touch.'

'I want very much. You good friend to me.' She wipes her eyes and smiles.

34

Mum has had three orders for cakes following the garden open day and is busy baking. I go next door to see Nav but he is out with Devi and I sit instead with Mrs Gayatri for a while and chat.

'The garden open day was wonderful,' she says. 'I know the idea was yours – thank you so much. And I am so happy that your health has improved so much.'

'So am I,' I tell her. 'I still have to be very careful not to overdo it. I hope I'm going to be able to cope back at school. I'm getting better now but I might get worse again. You never know with ME. I'm worried – but I'm also happy.'

'Yes – you must be careful, but you are so different to when you first brought that package round to me.'

'Your life is so different too,' I point out.

She smiles. 'Yes – I just had the birds to keep me company then,' she says, nodding. 'I am so happy to have Devi back in my life – and of course Nav too.

The stroke was a shock, but I am much stronger now – and if it hadn't happened maybe I would still be alone.'

She says she'll get Nav to knock for me when he gets back. I go home and I've only just taken off my shoes when the doorbell rings. I can't wait to tell Nav all about Reema. I open the door – and nearly jump in the air. I am so shocked. It isn't Nav. It's Marek!

'*Marek! Mum! It's Marek!*'

'Hi, sis!' he says, wriggling out of his rucksack and dumping it with a thud in the hallway, before throwing his arms round me.

'Not too tight!' I tell him as Mum rushes out into the hall. She's swearing in Polish.

'Oh, Marek!' she cries.

He lets go of me and hugs Mum.

'I thought it was time to come home,' he says.

'Come – sit in the kitchen. Have some cake! Tell us everything,' Mum demands.

We sit and listen while Marek tells us funny stories and asks us what we've been up to. I tell him about the open garden and about Reema.

'So good that you're not stuck upstairs any more,' he says.

Mum tells him how her cake business is starting to take off.

'I'm so happy you are home,' says Mum. 'But what are you going to do now? Will you go back to university?'

'Mum I don't want to,' he says, shaking his head. 'I hated it there. It wasn't right for me.'

'Your dad won't be happy,' Mum says, sighing.

'Will he throw me out?' Marek asks. 'I know how much I've disappointed him.'

'He wants the best for you, that's all,' says Mum. 'If you don't go back to studies, what will you do?'

'I know what I want to do,' says Marek, 'but I need to talk about it with Dad first.'

None of us are sure how Dad will react to Marek being back and we all hold our breath in trepidation when he comes through the front door later.

Mum rushes out to greet him. He suspects something immediately.

'What's going on?'

'Look who's here!' Mum says softly.

Marek steps out nervously from the kitchen. I am right behind him.

'Hello, Dad,' he says.

Dad stands open-mouthed. For once he says nothing. He seems lost for words.

'I'm back,' Marek tells Dad.

'What for?' Dad asks gruffly. 'You're returning to university?'

'No.' Marek shakes his head.

'What you back for then?' Dad demands. 'Money?'

'No, Dad – I want to work with you.'

'With me?' Dad is open-mouthed once more.

'Dad – I know you'd like me to study, but I want to learn a trade and work with you at the same time, like an apprentice. Maybe plumbing or something like that.'

'This is what you want?' Dad repeats, looking bemused.

Marek nods.

I am still tense, waiting for Dad to explode. I sense Mum is the same.

'OK,' says Dad, slapping Marek on the shoulder. 'Then that is what you will do.'

'Really, Dad?' Marek asks.

'Yes, son,' says Dad.

Nav is here. I'm on a high about Marek being home. Nav is still on a high from the success of his garden open day.

'So many came – we raised money for such a good cause!' he says. 'Maybe one day I will have a garden at the Chelsea Flower Show! What do you think?'

'Anything's possible!' I agree.

He smiles. Then he kisses me gently on the lips – and I feel a rushing sensation, as if the blood is suddenly whizzing round inside me.

'You know what? This has been quite a year,' he says. 'So much has happened that I never imagined – meeting Nani, moving here, a new school, the garden.' He pauses, then reaches out to touch my arm. 'Good things, but ordinary things. But you – there's nothing ordinary about what you did. Even with your illness, you saved a girl from slavery.'

I picure Reema – her sad face at the window and the contrast with her vibrant, hopeful eyes when I went to visit her.

Nav's hand is so soft on my arm. 'With your help,' I whisper.

'Her life is so much better now,' says Nav. His hand slides down and squeezes mine gently, 'and yours is about to get better too.'

'You mean going back to school?'

'No – not that.' He grins. 'I mean because of the hot guy next door! I mean you and me – us!'

'Oh – *that*!' I laugh, and I lean forwards and kiss him softly back.

I am not a ghost. I am flesh and blood. I am more flesh now that I eat good food. The ache of hunger inside me has gone. I am afraid but I have hope too. I have good people — my foster parents, my cousin, my friend Kasia. I will work hard at school. I hope I can stay in this country.

When I saw Kasia in the window I thought she was like me. She thought I was like her. We were both inside the house — never coming out. We were hidden, our stories never told. But now our lives have changed — we see the light. Like Kasia, I am no longer a girl in the window. I am a girl of many windows and many doors too.

AUTHOR'S NOTE

I have personal experience of ME/CFS which started in my 20s and seriously affected my life for the next ten years. I still have to be careful as symptoms do come back if I overdo it – but I value every aspect of the life I now lead, remembering a time when I didn't imagine I'd ever be well enough to get married and have a family.

ME/Chronic Fatigue Syndrome affects millions of people world-wide, approximately 250,000 in the UK, 21,000 of them children and teenagers. Many people recover after a period of months or years, but others remain ill and 25% are severely affected, with some bed bound for years. When I began to plan this book, I was shocked to see how little progress has been made in research as to the cause or treatment. Research in this area has been grossly underfunded. I hope more funding will be forthcoming and that progress will be made to help all affected with ME.

ACKNOWLEDGEMENTS

I want to start by thanking my family – and especially my husband Adam and our children Michael and Zoe, who I love so much.

I feel privileged to be published by Egmont who have looked after me so well! My editors Liz Bankes and Stella Paskins have been wonderful. I also have a brilliant agent in Anne Clark who helped me to develop the beginning of this idea into something that could become an actual book and helped me survive the ups and downs of writing with a deadline (a new experience!).

Many people helped me with the research for this novel – and I apologise if I have left anyone out. In particular I would like to thank Iwona Olejniczak, Raj Shah and Savita Kalhan for support with Polish and Hindu aspects; Action for ME, Jess Muxlow, Abbey, Michaela and many other young people with ME who answered my questions and/or gave feedback on the manuscript: the NSPCC whose staff were so helpful and Ann-Marie O'Keeffe for gardening advice.

I'd like to give a special mention to Jennifer

Brea, whose film 'Unrest' about her life with ME is incredibly powerful and from which I quoted at the start of the book. Anyone who wants to know more about life with ME should watch it.

I am also so grateful for the support of Janis Inwood, former librarian of Southgate School and Southgate School beta readers Sofia, Nina, Cameron and Naeemah; my Friday writing workshop members Angela Kanter, Jo Barnes, Vivien Boyes and Derek Rhodes – whose constructive feedback and emotional support has been, as ever, invaluable. I am grateful too for the support of City Lit where I began as a student and now teach adults who want to write for children and young people. It's a wonderful place to learn and to teach!

USEFUL CONTACTS

Action for ME
www.actionforme.org.uk

ME Association
www.meassociation.org.uk

NSPCC (National Society for the Prevention of Cruelty to Children)
www.nspcc.org.uk

Childline
www.childline.org.uk

Jemma knows who committed the murder.

She knows because he told her.

And she can't tell anyone.

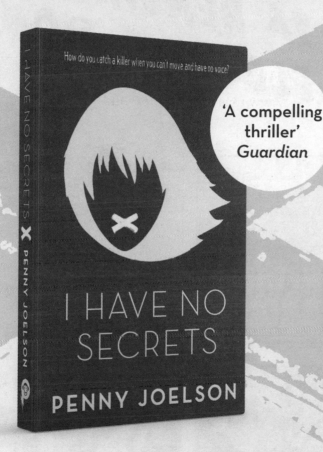

'A compelling thriller'
Guardian

Winner of the Worcestershire Teen Book Awards 2018
Winner of the Leeds Book Award 2018

HIGH VOLTAGE YA READING FROM ELECTRIC MONKEY

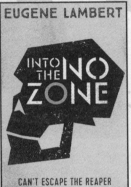

EUGENE LAMBERT

INTO THE NO ZONE

CAN'T ESCAPE THE REAPER

CAN YOU HANDLE REALITY?

THIS CARELESS LIFE

RACHEL McINTYRE

BORN SCARED

KEVIN BROOKS

WINNER OF THE CILIP CARNEGIE MEDAL

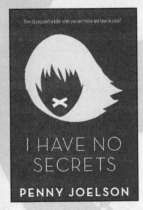

How do you catch a killer when you can't move and have no voice?

I HAVE NO SECRETS

PENNY JOELSON

DON'T LET ME FALL . . .

FLIGHT OF A STARLING

LISA HEATHFIELD

MICHAEL GRANT   NUMBER ONE BESTSELLING AUTHOR OF THE GONE SERIES

MONSTER

SUPERPOWERS DON'T ALWAYS MAKE YOU A HERO